This *Time* of DARKNESS

Don't get left behind!

STARSCAPE

Let the journey begin . . .

From the Two Rivers
  The Eye of the World: Part One
  by Robert Jordan

Ender's Game
  by Orson Scott Card

Mairelon the Magician
  by Patricia C. Wrede

Ender's Shadow
  by Orson Scott Card

Orvis
  by H. M. Hoover

Prince Ombra
  by Roderick MacLeish

A College of Magics
  by Caroline Stevermer

Deep Secret
  by Diana Wynne Jones

Hidden Talents
  by David Lubar

Obernewtyn
  by Isobelle Carmody

Song in the Silence
  by Elizabeth Kerner

To the Blight
  The Eye of the World: Part Two
  by Robert Jordan

The Cockatrice Boys
  by Joan Aiken

The Whispering Mountain
  by Joan Aiken

The Garden Behind the Moon
  by Howard Pyle

The Dark Side of Nowhere
  by Neal Shusterman

The Magician's Ward
  by Patricia C. Wrede

Pinocchio
  by Carlo Collodi

Another Heaven, Another Earth
  by H. M. Hoover

The Wonder Clock
  by Howard Pyle

The Shadow Guests
  by Joan Aiken

This Time of DARKNESS

H. M. Hoover

STARSCAPE

A TOM DOHERTY ASSOCIATES BOOK
NEW YORK

This is a work of fiction. All the characters and events portrayed in this book are either products of the author's imagination or are used fictitiously.

THIS TIME OF DARKNESS

Cover art by Patrick Farley

A Starscape Book
Published by Tom Doherty Associates, LLC
175 Fifth Avenue
New York, NY 10010

www.starscapebooks.com

ISBN: 0-765-34567-6

First Starscape edition: March 2003

Printed in the United States of America

0 9 8 7 6 5 4 3 2 1

For Rosie

———————————————————————————

This Time of
DARKNESS

1

It was day 157, and it was raining. Or at least Amy hoped it was. She could hear liquid running down the outside of the opaque wall. Of course a pipe could have broken up-level. They often did. The city was old.

"What are you staring at?" whispered Anita, who sat next to her.

"It's raining."

"So?"

Amy shrugged, intimidated by the older girl's lack of interest. "I'd like to see rain sometime . . . just to see what it's like."

"Who cares?" said Anita, who had no idea what rain was.

"Me."

"That figures."

Triggered by their whispers, the nearest camera swung around and aimed in their direction. Its red light blinked a warning. The watcher had seen them talking.

"You will have two hours to complete this test," the computer whispered through its thousand tiny speakers. "Begin at the bell tone." The computer asked a question requiring a one-word answer. The student said the word and pressed the button for the next question. When the final question was answered, the student could either signal for review and hear the questions again, or shut the terminal off, thus recording the score. Technology had eliminated the need to read or write. Boredom had eliminated the desire.

Amy finished the test in twelve minutes. She made four deliberate errors. She did not signal completion but waited, head bent as if still working. She had learned it did not pay to attract attention.

The learning center in which she sat was the size of a football field, grimy yellow, low-ceilinged, windowless, and dimly lit. Around her sat a thousand students, ranging in age from ten to sixteen, each with an "A" name, each at a terminal unit precisely thirty-one inches from the next. The room smelled of unwashed bodies, stale food, and musty walls. Next door was learning center B, and next to that was C, and so on down the line, all the same.

Bored with hearing the same questions over again, Amy sat up and cautiously glanced around. She could see Anita's throat working as the girl struggled to verbalize thought. In front of Anita sat Axel, curled in his seat, hugging himself and rocking, his eyes glazed. If he could hear the computer's voice in his speaker he gave no sign of it; he never spoke; his hands never touched his terminal board.

Amy saw nothing wrong with his behavior. A lot of kids were like him. Sometimes she wished she could be like them, or like anyone but herself. At least they fit in. Anita found learning difficult. School absorbed her completely, instead of boring her as it did Amy. Axel could shut everything out from the moment he entered the learning center. Only the dismissal bell seemed to release him.

Amy was always aware of the boredom, of being shut in with the constant murmur of the instructor's voice in a thousand speakers, of the whispers and restless shifting of the students, and of the watcher's cameras. Sometimes she wondered what was wrong with her; no one else seemed to find fault with their life. Or if they did, they kept quiet about it. As she did. Maybe there were a lot of people like her, and she just never knew them. And maybe there weren't.

Propping her head on her left hand, she stared unseeingly at her screen while she passed the time daydreaming. Her favorite daydream was "going outside." She would imagine what it was like outside the city—a place with no walls and no ceilings, no hallways or ramps—maybe even no people— or less—

Halfway down the room she saw a boy get up and leave. A girl followed, then another boy. She waited for five more students to leave before shutting off her own terminal. Anita hissed, "Show-off," at her as she left. Axel stopped rocking and sat up.

In the control room the watcher frowned. By chance he had been watching Amy when she first looked up from her screen. Experience as well as instinct told him she had finished the test—which indicated too-quick comprehension.

He asked the computer for her life file: Age eleven, born on level nine, mother food prep tech, father unknown. No physical or mental dysfunctions. No recorded deviations. The only mark against the child was literacy. No record of who had taught her to read and write. Literacy was not an official crime, but it was an affectation of superiority which the government tried to discourage among the lower levels, since it often led to unacceptable behavior. He noted that corrective programming had brought her down to mid-normal and kept her there. Or had she kept herself there? That was a possibility; the too-bright could mimic normalcy.

The watcher weighed fact against instinct. Instinct won. He coded her file as that of a potential troublemaker and returned to scanning in time to see Axel, the transfer from twelve, give his terminal a savage kick before running from the room. The exit camera saw Axel pause in the hall, looking for someone. In that unguarded moment the boy's expression changed from apathy to hope.

Perhaps the child was not going psycho but pretending? The watcher hesitated. In a job like this, one had to guard against paranoia. When these brats grew up and caused problems, the top levels could always say, "Why wasn't this spotted years ago?" and then his neck would be on the line. God, how he hated kids!

Axel caught up with Amy at the corner. An emergency car was coming, sirens screaming, the sound trapped and echoing against the low ceiling. Amy had stopped to put on her earguards. He touched her arm and, when she turned, smiled his sweet, sad smile. Then, as the noise got painfully loud, his eyes left hers and he seemed to retreat into himself. His lips began to move.

Thinking he was talking to her, she slid back an earguard and leaned closer; in the voice of a small child, he was singing a lullaby. "Rufus the Rabbit is going to sleep. Down in his burrow where silence is deep."

It was close and hot in the hall, but Amy shivered. She put her hands over his ears as tightly as she could and held them there until the siren was far down the hall.

It was hard to stand that way. The crowd was thick, and people jostled past the stationary little island formed by the pair. Some people bumped accidentally; others deliberately hit one child or the other and quickly disappeared in the crowd. Amy took blows for granted. She had been taught that people expressed their hostility or their need to touch in the hallways. It did not pay to stand still.

"Come on," she said, releasing him. "Let's go home." He didn't answer, but he had stopped singing, and his eyes focused again. She started across the corridor, and he followed.

"Why didn't you take the test?"

"Why should I?" he said. "They don't care what you know—so long as you don't cause problems."

Amy thought that over and decided there was some truth to it. Still, "If you don't answer some questions, even wrong, they notice you. And then you get special programming."

A nearby litter vac turned on just then, and the roar drowned her out. Loose garbage flew toward the suction screen, and Amy squinted against the dust. Axel's face went blank with the noise, and the corners of his mouth twitched.

"Why don't you wear your earguards?" she yelled over the roar.

"I don't have any."

She stared at him. "Why not?"

Two men brushed between them and nearly knocked them down. Neither pair looked at the other.

"I don't know how to get them."

He was a little abnormal, she decided. Everyone knew how to get necessities. "You take your ID card to the depot, stand in line, put your card in the slot, tell the machine you want earguards, and the earguards come down the chute."

Axel looked at her for a moment and then at the pavement. The floor was cracked and rough here; litter had collected in the cracks, and he stepped over them with exaggerated care. But he didn't say anything.

The heavy scent of a fry shop filled the corridor, and Amy was distracted by her stomach's growl. She didn't really like deep-fried vegetable peelings, but they were hot and salty. Sometimes they were even crisp. And when she was hungry, she wished she could afford them. But it didn't pay to think about what you couldn't have.

"Do you have an ID card?"

Axel nodded. He looked scared.

He stopped walking and leaned against the wall. Amy hesitated before turning back to join him. "What's wrong?"

He didn't answer. After a few seconds she was tired of being jostled while she stood still.

"You're going to get your back all greasy from that filthy wall," she warned him. "Also roaches on you."

He jumped as if he had received an electric shock, turned and stared at the wall. It was sticky with years of grime. At least a dozen roaches clung there, antennae quivering as they fed. More were on the pavement.

"How do you live this way?" His voice was almost a whisper, and she had to ask him to repeat the question. "How can people stand it?" He looked as if he were going to be sick. "The noise and crowds and dirt—it's all dark and dirty!"

"It's like that everywhere," Amy said, puzzled, "everywhere I've ever been. Is it different on level twelve?" For a moment hope glimmered. If it was, level twelve wasn't that far up—maybe she could go visit him.

"It's just as bad. Worse where I sleep."

Hope flickered out. "So why did you ask?"

"Because it's—" He cast a worried glance at the wall. "Can we talk while we walk?"

"Do you want to go get earguards or not?"

"Yes. If you come with me."

"You *do* have your ID?"

"Yes."

"Come on then. The nearest depot's down this block."

The supply depot was crowded with long lines at every chute. Axel no more than stepped inside than he wanted out.

"We'll be here a long time," he said, edging toward the door. She grabbed him by the arm and saw his eyes were beginning to go blank. He was about to shut everything out. Her first impulse was to leave him there; then she remembered him singing when the siren went by.

She took his hand and held it. "I hate crowds, too," she said. "But we can stand it for as long as it takes."

"I'm O.K." He pulled free, then looked at her. "No, I'm not," he admitted and took her hand again. "Talk to me. It's easier if I don't have to think about where I am."

Amy didn't understand that remark but did as he asked. She whispered her suspicions that it was raining outside. When he nodded agreement—instead of sneering as Anita had—she found herself liking him in spite of his oddness.

The two of them stood there talking in their city-issue clothing—shapeless shirts and pants of dark brown. The color did not show the dirt. The dark cloth made their faces pale and their eyes look much too large. Their hair was cut to regulation standards, a bowl cut with bangs that accented Amy's round face, while Axel's fine nose and chin were reduced to fox-like sharpness. Their shoes were thong sandals, thick-soled and clumsy, and their bare feet were filthy. They looked no worse than anyone else.

"It's nice when it rains," Axel said, his voice wistful. "I didn't used to think so, but I do now. It's not like the irrigation mist. Rain comes in drops. All different sizes and speeds. Sometimes, when the wind blows, it rains so hard the roof sings—"

"You got some line of garbage, kid." A man in line in

front of Axel had turned around and was looking down at the boy. The man's voice was heavy with contempt. "You never seen rain. You never been outside. You never gonna get outside. So can the crap."

"Maybe he comes from level eighty and he's slumming?" A woman joined in. "Maybe he's a midget CS-fifty in disguise?"

Both adults laughed.

Axel blushed and his chin touched his chest.

"No one can go outside," another man told the boy, not with hostility, but in an effort to correct wrong thinking. "You're old enough to know that. Besides, there's nothing to do out there. There's no reason to go there."

Axel risked a glance at the man and quickly looked away but said nothing. Amy didn't blame him for not defending himself. It didn't pay to provoke strange adults. Some of them hit you, and there were never any guards around when you needed them. Like Axel she kept her head down and her mouth shut until the adults grew bored with staring at them.

The lines moved forward slowly. She passed the time wondering if Axel did know what he was talking about. He sounded as if he did. She could hardly wait to get out of the depot to question him. Because sometime she was going to go outside, she decided. She was going to see for herself.

2

"What's on level eighty?" Axel asked as soon as they got out of the depot.

"Put on your earguards."

"Then I can't hear you."

"Leave one side up." She pointed to her head. "Like mine. When the noise gets loud, turn the cup down." She frowned at him. "How come you don't know that?"

He shrugged. "What's on level eighty—am I supposed to know that, too?"

"No," she said. "Just maybe heard stories about it. I don't really know if there is an eightieth level—or even a thirtieth for real."

"What stories?"

"Little kid stories about how, if you're good, you'll get to go up there to this special place where everything is clean and light and there are no rats or roaches. The people who run things, the authorities, are supposed to live up there and have walls you can see through. They can see the sky and a whole lot of water called the ocean."

Now she had Axel's attention. In all the time she'd known him, she'd never seen him look so interested. It changed his whole face. He looked almost bright. Encouraged by this response, she elaborated.

"They say there's real sunlight up there and places where there's no ceiling where grass and trees and flowers are. Real stuff. Alive—none of it synthetic."

"People have seen this?" He pulled her to a halt and shook her with both hands. "They've been there?"

"Don't get so excited—people are looking at us." She freed a hand and pulled him along. "No. Nobody I know ever *saw* it. It's just a story. I don't know anybody who's ever been more than five levels from their apartment in their whole life. There's no reason to go. The city is so big—and every level is the same. . . ." She was automatically quoting the words the teaching machines recited over and over.

She remembered what she wanted to talk about. "How come you know so much about rain?" Maybe he had her book—or any book?

He looked around to see if anyone was listening and then said, "I don't want to talk about that any more."

"Were you just telling a story? Because I need to know."

Axel reached up and turned his earguard down. He'd learned a new way to shut people out. Seeing him do that, she thought he'd turn at the next block and head off up-ramp toward the youth shelter where he stayed, but he didn't. He walked all the way home with her. He'd never done that before.

The entry to Amy's place was next door to a fry shop. The main passageway and the ten cross passages all smelled of stale cooking oil. The security screen showed the passages empty, except for a man sleeping off a high in the third hall on the right. Amy often saw him there; he had never bothered anyone, so she went in.

"Why are all the crazies naked?" Axel pointed at the sleeping man.

"The rats chew the food spots off their clothes while the crazies sleep," she explained. "If they put their clothes under them, the rats can't get at them so easily."

"Oh."

White noise from the vent fans seemed to make the warren quieter. There was a door every fifteen feet along each passage. All looked alike and all were locked.

Amy counted to herself. "Third hall, left, five doors down on the right," and pressed her hand against the fingerprint lock. The lock clicked and the door screeched open over its worn track.

"There's nobody in there." Axel smiled with genuine pleasure as he saw the room. "How lucky you are!"

Amy nodded. "It's just me and Valory, my mother. There's room for one more, but the Housing Authority probably forgot that so we have the place to ourselves."

"Lucky! Where's your mother?"

"At work. She's the texture expert in this sector's food prep lab. She gets back at three, but sometimes she visits people and doesn't get back till late."

Amy did not think it necessary to add that her mother forbade her to bring people home. Axel would be long gone before Valory came back.

"And you get to be alone here?"

When she nodded, he said again, "Lucky!" She liked that; everyone else she knew said, "Aren't you scared to be alone?" She wasn't but she knew most people were.

The door shut behind Axel as he stood studying the room. Amy's home was six and one half feet high and fifteen feet square. Its pink paint was dark with age and grime. On one wall the sanit module flanked the micro-cooker and freezer; on the opposite wall was a bunk bed with brown blankets. Hooks held clothing. A small table, two cable spools that served as stools, and a crudely built shelf completed the furnishings. There were no windows, pictures, or rug. Light came from a narrow ceiling panel, entertainment from a cracked vu-screen, now turned off, heat and ventilation from two mesh-screened ceiling vents.

"No camera?" he asked. Amy shook her head, and he seemed visibly to relax. "The shelter has them. All over." He sat down on one of the stools and pushed his earguards back.

"How do you know about rain?" Amy got right to the point.

"How do you?"

It was her turn to evade. "I just do."

"But how?"

"I read about it." She waited for the contempt that should follow this confession. All she got from Axel was interest.

"Where?"

"In a . . . uh . . . book."

For once he looked directly at her. "I never saw books here . . . are you allowed to have them?"

"There's no law against it," Amy said, puzzled by his use of "you" instead of "we." Did he feel that isolated? "There's no law—but if they know you have one, the authorities take it away. They say that books are old and dirty and a sanitary risk. They don't like us to read. . ."

"Yeah.'" Axel's expression was funny again. "I noticed."

"Can you read?"

"Do you have books?"

"Not any more." She turned and sat down on the lower bunk and pretended to brush something off her toes. Then she brushed her hair away from her eyes. The question reminded her of a bad time in her life, a time she didn't like to think about when anybody else was around because she might cry.

Until Amy had been eight years old, she and Valory had shared their apartment with an old woman named Janet. It had been Janet's apartment before the authorities forced her to share it. The old woman had cared for Amy and in doing so secretly taught the girl to read and write. Hidden in the litter she had accumulated in her life was her only precious possession, a book. It was a partial copy, dirty and battered, of an ancient, one-volume children's encyclopedia. But for Amy, Janet and that old book opened windows on a world neither had ever seen and which Janet warned might not even exist any more. "But it's nice to think about." When she died, Janet promised, the book would be Amy's, but only if Amy promised that when she grew up she would teach another child to read and write. Amy had promised.

But Janet died one day while Amy was at the learning center, and the girl came home to find both the old woman and her possessions gone. The loss had left an emptiness in Amy's life that nothing seemed to fill.

"If I tell you something, promise you won't tell anyone?" Axel said.

Amy hesitated; she no longer made promises lightly. "If it's dangerous, I don't want to know."

"It's not, because no one believes me. They think it just proves I'm psycho. But it's true. Can I tell you?" When she still didn't say yes, he added, "It explains how I know about rain."

"How?"

"Because I come from outside."

It wasn't the answer she expected. And yet, while her mouth fell open with shock, she believed him. It was weird, but if true, it might explain a lot of things about him—all the things he didn't know, the stupid questions he asked, his fear of things that sane people took for granted. But it was impossible—or was it? She wanted to believe, if only for the hope belief offered.

"What does the city look like from the outside?"

"I don't know. I—" He saw her expression and hurried to say, "I came in on the freight belt—in a vegetable bin. I didn't see anything—"

"What's fratebelt?"

"It's how the city gets its food and dumps its garbage—"

"I never heard of it," she said firmly. "If you got in, why didn't you go back out again?"

"I tried!" He was suddenly very close to tears, staring at the wall but seeing something else. His body twisted on the stool. "I hunted and hunted and I couldn't find the way back! It's all dark tunnels and ramps and machinery! And it's hot and stinks so bad! I was scared and lost, and men chased me—"

Every city child grew up hearing bogeymen stories about the people who roamed the service levels down below.

"Did they have pasty skin and long white hair and fangs and fingernails like claws?" Amy wanted to know.

"No." Her question startled the boy out of his memory. "They're filthy dirty, and they've got sores all over, and—" He shut his eyes and shook his head until his fine hair whipped around his face. "I'm not going to think about them any more."

"O.K." Amy sighed with disappointment; he had just described an average crazy. She'd always enjoyed those terrible stories. Yet the fact that Axel didn't confirm them strengthened his claim. If he'd never been down there, she decided, he would have agreed with her story just to please her. "Why don't you tell me about outside and why you wanted to come here?"

"I never wanted to come! It was an accident. We were exploring down by the freight tracks, Ty and Margo and me. We aren't supposed to play down there because of all the equipment . . . but we found a hole in the fence big enough to squeeze through and so we did. We were looking around . . . there wasn't much to see—just row after row of empty bins standing on the shuntways—only one track moves at a time," he added by way of explanation for Amy's benefit.

Amy had no idea what he was talking about. She had never seen anything like this and couldn't picture what it looked like. But Axel looked better now that he was talking. She'd never heard him talk much. "Who are Ty and Margo?" she asked.

"Friends. They live where I used to live." He took a deep breath. "So, anyhow, we were exploring, and one of the shuntways came on, and the bins started to move down to the terminal for loading. And Ty and Margo got scared because the bin carriers are so big and look like they move by themselves. If you got in front of one of them they'd mash you like a potato. So they wanted to leave, and we started back toward the hole in the fence, but the moving line cut off the way we had come in and we had to detour up and over another line. When I got to the top of the bin I was climbing, the view was pretty good—I could see all over the yard—and I stood up there looking around while the other two climbed down. Then, just to see if I could do it, I jumped to the next bin. I must have hit some switch when I landed because the bin lid tipped up and I fell in like a lettuce. I remember looking up and seeing the lid shut out the sky, and then my head hit the wall."

"Then what happened?"

He reached up with both hands and felt his head. "This." The boy's hair hid a nasty red scar that zigzagged from behind his left ear to the top of his head. "I've never seen it, but it still hurts when I press it or they cut my hair."

Amy made sympathetic noises. "The medic did a stinking job," she said. "I never saw a scar that bad."

"Wasn't the medic's fault." Axel pushed his hair back in place and scratched an itch on his neck. "When I woke it was dark and I was buried under cabbages and the bin was moving."

"What did you do?"

"Nothing—except decide I was going to die. The cabbages were so heavy I couldn't move. It was hard to breathe—I hurt all over—except I couldn't feel a lot of me. I tried to sleep but I was too cold. The next thing I remember was falling again. I thought I was dreaming it over—" He shivered and rubbed his arms.

"The bin had come into the warehouse here and dumped its load. I was on the bottom so I tumbled out on top. When I could see, I crawled off the cabbages and onto a walkway. I didn't know where I was, and I called for help but nobody came. It's all automatic. So I just kept walking and falling down and going through every door I found, trying to get outside or find people—and then I was sorry I found them—"

He fell silent for a moment. "They took my clothes and my shoes . . . the one who took my shoes must have felt guilty or something because he went away and then came back and dragged me to a ramp and pressed an alarm and ran. I would have run too, but I couldn't move any more."

"And the authorities came and took you to the hospital?"

He nodded.

"And they didn't believe you?"

He shook his head. "Nobody listened. When someone did finally—the man who changed the bandage on my head—he just laughed and said he didn't blame me for making up a story like that after how the crazies beat me up—he'd make up a story too if he was simple enough to go down there. And when I said it was true, he quit laughing and played my hospital record and told me *that* was the truth and I should remember it."

"What did it say?"

He shrugged. "I don't know. . . ." His voice dropped to nothing as he confessed. "That I was a crazy. Every time I told them how I got here they gave me something that made me sleep. Finally I quit trying and just said, yes, they were right. I got tired of sleeping."

"And they sent you to the youth shelter?"

Again came the quick nod. "Is it a crime to not come from the city?" he asked.

Amy thought that over. "Everybody does," she said finally.

"Well, is it a crime to want to get out?"

"I think so. They say there's nothing outside any more, and the air is too polluted to breathe—"

"They told me that too, but it's not true—maybe it was a long time ago, but people live outside. There are three hundred people in Mercer, the town I come from, and—"

The door slid open to reveal a small, plump woman dressed in beige fatigues. Her face, almost bovinely placid, did not change when she saw Axel. "Are you here by authority?" she asked Axel.

"No . . ."

"I invited him. He's a friend from—"

"You are in my space. Get out!" The woman stepped aside and pointed out the door.

Without a glance at Amy, the boy left, dodging past the adult as if he expected to be hit.

3

The woman's eyes followed the boy, but she made no move until the door closed behind him. Then, like an animal who has successfully routed an intruder from its burrow, she grunted and put the food canister she carried into the freezer.

"Did he drink water or flush the sanit?" She did not look at Amy.

"No. We just talked."

"He didn't use water?"

"No."

"Water costs. Waste costs."

"I know." Amy had heard this litany too often to listen

now, when her mind was busy with Axel's story. She was considering going after him. But that would be pointless. It was shift change; the halls would be jammed with people. Even if she went up to the shelter on level twelve, there wouldn't by any place where they could talk privately.

"Why did you let him in?" The woman persisted.

"We were talking. I thought it would be O.K."

Amy did not resent these questions. All the adults she knew were very possessive of their private space; Valory was no different. People were like that when they got older.

"Don't do it again."

"Can't we even talk in here?"

"No." Valory turned on the vu-screen. "It's time for my meditation show. You go out."

On the screen a circle of pale blue light glowed, its roundness distorted by the crack. The circle faded. A cartoon character, an androgynous knob-headed little person, filled the screen. "I lose my Self in my work," it said. "My work sets me free. My work makes me important. I do the best I can." Its little mouth smiled. "When I work I do not see or hear those around me. They are working, too." The little body took itself to an assembly line where other little characters smiled as they worked.

Valory smiled too, so absorbed in the screen that her eyes never left it as she stepped out of her thongs and stretched out on the lower bunk. She lay there watching, her lips moving as the cartoon characters spoke. There was something in the woman's expression that reminded Amy of Axel when he hugged himself and rocked. The woman saw her watching and said, "Go out. I can't think if you're here."

"I buy things because buying makes me happy." The knob-head smiled. "Things never disappoint. Only people disappoint." Valory nodded silent agreement.

Amy had seen this show a dozen times and thought it was simple enough to bore a roach. But she never said so because it was a very popular show and everybody loved it. "You're not normal enough to appreciate it," Valory had said once when Amy asked her why people watched it. "That old woman spoiled your mind. It's not your fault, but don't say stupid things like that in public. You make me look bad." Since then Amy had kept her opinions to herself. It didn't pay to let people know you didn't think the way they did.

She went out, intending to sit outside the door, as she always did when The Show was on. But when she got outside, Axel was sitting on the floor at the end of the hall.

"I thought you left," she said, glad to see him.

"No . . . I hoped you'd come out. I didn't mean to get you in trouble."

"You didn't." Amy kicked two roaches out of the way and sat down beside him.

"I hate those things!"

"Roaches? Me, too. But they're all over—they're very old insects—almost the oldest there are. That's because they're good mothers and choose a warm dry nest and take care of their babies until the babies can find food themselves." She grinned at him. "Of course baby roaches grow up fast."

"Is that true?"

She nodded. "I read that. Tell me about outside now."

"For one thing, we don't have all these roaches . . . and . . ." He looked sideways at her, then at the floor, then stared at the opposite wall. "I don't know where to begin. It's a lot different from this."

"Start anywhere." His hesitation aroused her doubts again, and she crossed her fingers in the hope that his whole story so far had not been a lie. For if it was true, then Janet had been right and there was another way to live—

"It's sunny," he began hesitantly, "most days anyhow. And the land is flat where we live—but we can see the hills. And unless the machines are working the fields near town, it's very quiet—you can hear crickets and the dogs barking at night—"

"What's dogs?" Amy interrupted. She wasn't sure what sunny or crickets meant either but didn't want to look completely ignorant.

"There's grass—all kinds of plants and trees—" He stopped and stared at her. "Dogs?" he repeated. "Just plain dogs—four-legged animals with fur and tails—"

"Like rats?"

"Bigger—you never saw a dog?"

She shook her head. An occupant passed on his way home, and they fell silent until his apartment door closed.

"How about a cat?"

"Is that an animal too?" she asked and saw a bewildered expression come over him. "What's wrong?"

"Nothing—you're not going to understand a lot of what I tell you. And then you'll think I'm making it all up."

"No, I won't! Go on—try me."

Axel took a deep breath; he seemed discouraged by her ignorance and a little contemptuous. She rather resented that—how did he think people felt sometimes when he asked the questions he asked?

"We raise chickens—you know what a chicken is? You should—we ship zillions of them to the city—all ready to eat"—he paused to think—"but I never tasted chicken here. Just that slop they call chic-tex."

"That's good stuff!" Amy said. "It's the best food the lab makes."

Axel made a face. "You think that's good? It's yeast and soybeans they make taste like rotten chicken. Not real meat at all." He shifted into lotus position and flicked a bug off his knee. "Where does the good food go once it comes into the city?"

"People eat it?" suggested Amy, who had always thought all food came from the food labs like the one where her mother worked.

"I've been here a long time—months maybe," Axel said. "I haven't tasted real food in all that time—except cabbage cooked with no salt. But all we do is raise food and ship it into the city. Where does it go?"

"Maybe it gets lost in the lower levels—like you did?" said Amy. "Or the people down there eat it—"

"Or maybe it all goes to the eightieth level?"

"That's just a story." Amy was tired of being sidetracked on this subject. "Tell me about outside—forget about food," she ordered, but what he suggested stuck in her mind. Maybe her mother would know.

In the passageway across from them the sleeping man groaned, then rolled over and curled into fetal position. He was so thin his bones seemed to stick through his skin.

"Can he hear us?" asked Axel, worried. "He looks like he moved closer."

"No. We're talking low, and the fans cover it," Amy said. "Besides, he's crazy anyhow. Go on, tell me about outside."

Axel told her as much as he could about the world he claimed to be his. Much of what he said made no sense to her, but what she did grasp confirmed all Janet had suspected—there was still a place that was not city!

As she listened, what had been a daydream became an ambition. If such a place existed, she was going to go there. How she was to go about it was something she would figure out later.

According to Axel, almost everyone lived in cities; a lot of outside was something called deserted where nothing could live except a few plants. He hadn't seen that part because he was in the freight tunnel in a bin, but he had heard about it. And some was ocean, like the level-eighty stories said. He'd never seen that either. Where he lived was called the green-belt. His people tended the equipment in the place where food was grown for the cities. She didn't understand why or how they did this, but that didn't matter.

"Why do we all have to live in the city?" she wondered aloud.

"I'm not sure, but maybe there wouldn't be room enough outside to grow food if they let you out," Axel replied. "These people take up a lot of space—and they'd get in the way of the machines probably. And they're dirty—"

"Only because water is so scarce." Amy took that last remark personally. "I'd wash a lot more if I was allowed."

"There's a lot of water outside." The boy stretched out his arms and looked at them. They were dirty, but not half so dirty as his hands. "I don't know why it's scarce in here. I hate this place!" He wrapped his arms around himself and hunched over in misery.

"Is everything better outside?"

He nodded. He seemed depressed.

"Then let's go there! I always wanted to go . . . well, not always, but for a long time. When I was little I wanted to walk up to the eightieth level—just keep climbing ramps until I got there. But I don't believe in that story any more—not very much anyway."

"Why not?"

"Because. If everyone is equal and all levels are the same—and if one level lived like that—other people would notice it and want to go there, too. Wouldn't they?"

"If they could," agreed Axel. "If they knew about it."

"And even if there is an eightieth level it's still inside the city and I'd rather go out."

"Where's ground level?" He saw her puzzlement and explained, "Where the building meets the surface?"

"Level one?" That seemed logical to her.

But Axel shook his head. "I've been all over there. There's no outside door at all. There's none on two or three, either. A lot of this place is underground. All the freight belts are."

"How do you know that?" asked Amy.

"Because they come into our terminal at Mercer from tunnels, and they go back into tunnels—and the tunnels to the city all slant down. I saw them that day—"

In the dim passage across the way the man abruptly sat up and stared at them. By chance Amy glanced up to see him avert his stare. The man didn't look psycho—or drugged—not when you looked closely. Sick maybe, but not crazy. She watched him fumble around beneath himself, pull out a flattened bunch of rags and slowly dress. All the time he dressed he kept looking over at them. He began to talk to himself.

"What's wrong with him?" Axel sat up, ready to run.

"I don't know—if he comes near we'll go into my place."

The man rose with effort and kept one hand on the wall for support as he came toward the main passage, where he paused and looked both ways before starting toward the entrance. "The watcher is everywhere," they heard him say as he stumbled out of sight.

"He heard us!" Axel started to get up, but Amy pulled him down.

"He couldn't have. He's just trying to scare us. He probably thinks he's being funny."

"Maybe not." Axel was worried. "There are cameras everywhere, and in the shelter they say half the crazies are watchers in disguise—"

"And half the cameras are broken and some of them are dummy units," Amy said. "Crazies stare because they are crazies. If you start worrying about it all, you'll go crazy yourself."

"Yeah," Axel said quietly. "Sometimes when I see people like that, I think that's what I'll be when I grow up if I can't get out of here. . . ."

It hadn't occurred to Amy to think of crazies as once having been someone like herself or Axel . . . who grew up. It was a very scary idea. To have that as a future . . . Valory thought Amy's mind was spoiled already. What if others did, too?

"You don't have to worry about that," she said. "Not yet, anyway. We're going to get out of the city."

"When are we going to go?"

"I don't know—but we won't tell anybody, and we won't ask people questions. It doesn't pay to make people curious about why you want to know something."

"How will we do it? I've tried and—"

"I don't know. But there has to be a way."

4

Before going to sleep that night, Amy tried to picture the city in her mind. Her image was that of a labyrinth of halls and corridors, low-ceilinged, dim, busy with human life and noise. But she could not see an outer shape, an encasement and end to it all. Yet she knew there had to be one somewhere. People had come inside from somewhere.

The teaching machines said there were eighty levels and all levels were the same. Two wide corridors passed through each level. They were labeled A and B. Halls crossed the corridors. People lived in the blocks along the halls and worked in labs or factories on the corridors.

There was a saying: "Halls are straight and have an end; corridors go on forever." For all Amy knew, that was true. Every hall she'd ever walked ended eventually in a shop or living space. She'd explored a hundred and forty blocks of corridor A before turning back, and ninety blocks on B, and both had stretched on ahead, unchanging.

Once, Janet had told her, there had been open spaces between building sectors, high windowed lobbies that went up twenty levels or more, and moving ramps, and trees, and flowers. But that was long ago, Amy knew, and all gone now. Maybe it had been better then.

In the bunk below, Valory mumbled in her sleep and then thumped the wall as she rolled over and took a deep sighing breath. Amy put her earguards down; it was time for the woman to go into deep sleep, and when she did that, she ground her teeth. The girl hated that sound, a furtive *skeech-skeech-skeech*—like rats chewing inside the walls.

The bunk shook and Amy's eyes flew open to see the light flickering in the ceiling panel. The entire room was quaking with vibration from somewhere. She held her breath until the light became steady again. The shaking was normal. It happened most nights about this time and went on all night. But Amy always worried the lights might go out and there would be only blackness. Some people, she knew, prayed to their light panel and pasted bright things on the ceiling near it to encourage it to glow.

She had tried doing that, but Valory made her stop. It showed no faith in the authorities, Valory said, and you had to believe *they* were in control. Otherwise you got nowhere.

Now Amy reached over and pressed her palm flat against

the wall to feel the hum that never stopped. Although no one had ever told her so, she believed that so long as the wall hummed, so long as there was noise, the city was alive and the people in it were safe.

The light flickered again, and she closed her eyes. If the lights went out, she didn't want to know about it until she woke up. She went back to thinking.

The trouble was, she didn't know where to begin to look for a way out—or how long it would take to find it. If it took only a day, then she wouldn't have to worry about food and things like that. But if it took longer, where would she sleep at night? Sleeping in the halls was dangerous. And if she used her ID card for food, they could trace her and bring her back as a runaway. Then Valory would be angry and Amy would be labeled a troublemaker and have to wear orange suits and maybe get sent to Rehabilitation for chemotherapy and truth teaching.

She didn't want to cause her mother more shame or get her in trouble. If she'd been a normal child she would have been transferred to live in a training dorm as other ten-year-olds were, but she was eleven and the authorities still had not transferred her. Valory said it was because they didn't want Amy perverting other children with her reading.

If she went away, Amy thought, Valory would be glad because then the authorities might give permission for Valory's friend Ted to move in. The two adults often told Amy that if it weren't for her living here, things would be a lot easier for them. So she would give them the gift of her space.

She fell asleep feeling noble and a little sorry for herself, since she suspected that if she went away no one would miss her. Not only that, but they might be glad she'd gone.

Still, she didn't want to cause worry or have the authorities start looking for her as soon as she left. She would have to think of some excuse to be away. . . .

The slam of the sanit door woke her. Her earguards had slipped off, and the sudden noise frightened her and set her heart racing. She could never understand how her mother could get the sanit door to make that much noise—Amy had tried sliding it as hard as she could and never got more than a soft clunk out of it. But then Valory could make almost anything slam.

Soon I won't have to hear that any more, Amy thought, listening to the sounds from the module. Maybe never again. If I left today—her stomach suddenly felt lead-filled and she shivered. What if they did get outside and it was awful out there like people said it was and they couldn't get back in? Then what?

If you do find a way, you can stand inside and look out and see, her common sense told her. If it's bad, you don't have to go out; you can come back here. But what if Ted had moved into her space while she was gone?

This would not do. If she started thinking this way, she would give up before she started—as Axel had nearly given up. As the crazies had given up. Or she'd become like Valory. Amy wasn't sure what was wrong with her mother, but she knew she didn't want to be like her or, for that matter, like any adult she had ever known. Except Janet.

The sanit door rumbled open. Amy feigned sleep as Valory emerged to dress and comb her hair. Prolonged forced intimacy had created an aversion between them that increased as Amy got older. With her eyes shut, she knew every move Valory made.

She listened to the morning ritual until the noises indicated her mother's near departure for her job. Then she half sat up under the low ceiling.

"I nearly forgot to tell you," Amy said. "I'm going to ask to be moved into a training dorm."

The woman stared at the piece of protomush she was eating for breakfast. "They won't take you." She spoke without looking at the girl.

"They might. My record's pretty normal now. I can try."

"They won't take you," her mother repeated. "I know."

"You tried to get me moved out of here?"

"For the past year. For your own good. You should have a skill. Besides"—the tone became defensive—"I have a right to have some adult male company while I'm still young."

It was one thing to want to leave, but quite another to realize she definitely was not wanted and hadn't been for a long, long time. Amy found she was both surprised and frightened by her mother's words. But she wasn't going to let Valory know that.

"I'm going to apply myself," she said, "so if you come back and I'm not here—that's where I'll be."

"No such luck."

"What does that mean?"

"It means I'm going to be late for work if I don't quit listening to your stupid talk."

She rose and put the remains of her meal into the freezer, then without a further word went out the door. Neither of them said good-bye, but then, Amy thought later, strangers usually don't.

The girl climbed down from her bunk and stood in the middle of the tiny room, looking at it. This room was the only home she could remember. It was an odd feeling to think she might never see it again. It suddenly seemed a very safe place to be. Except she wasn't wanted here.

Although it wasn't her day to shower, she did so—half in

defiance and half from an urge to start out clean. Before she dressed, she opened the freezer and, finding six protomush disks there, put them all into the cooker and set the timer for an extra minute to make them dry, like cookies. She put on both of her two clean suits, one on top of the other, and when the mush was done, ate one cake. When the rest were cool, she slid them into her shirt pockets. In the baggy unpressed garments, bulging pockets made no difference. There was nothing else she wanted to take with her but her comb and toothbrush. She didn't own anything else. Turning on the roach ray, she policed the area. Keeping the room neat was her job, and she did it extra thoroughly.

When the blankets had been folded on each bunk mattress, the ray shut off, and, the dead bugs kicked out into the hall, she was finished with the room. There was no sign that she lived here except for her dirty sandals by the door. She washed them and put them in the micro-cooker to dry before putting them on, and then she left.

5

The crazy wasn't sleeping in his usual spot this morning. On her way out she saw him leaning against the fry shop window, shirt off, talking to himself. For a split second their glances met, and she felt a twinge of guilty fear. What if he was a watcher? But he looked away and drooled, and she promptly forgot about him as she entered the pedestrian traffic in the hallway.

She took for granted the dimly lit halls and corridors, concrete tunnels fetid with the scents of unwashed bodies, morning breaths, stale food odors, clogged drains, and ventilators blocked with refuse. This was normal for her. She had never known anything else.

Morning traffic was heavy with first-shift workers going to work, third-shifters coming home, and students en route to class. Delivery pushcarts blocked half the halls and crowded the corridors and ramps. The delivery people tended to get nasty when someone was in their way. Deliveries were supposed to be made at night but somehow never were.

The corridors were five times wider than the halls but worse to travel because of inter-level traffic, especially around the ramps. People were often knocked down and stepped on in the crush when the traffic lights changed. When that happened, sirens and guard whistles shrilled through the crowd roar. In the enclosed spaces all sounds echoed and were magnified over and over.

Amy had learned to walk as fast as traffic allowed, dodging and weaving to avoid all contact with strangers. People were odd in the anonymity of crowds; some hit and some caressed, and she was not sure which kind of touch was more frightening. Shut into the whispering protection of her earguards, she slipped through the mob with the swiftness of a wild thing, adept at eluding any kind of capture. Her walk to the learning center took her twenty-five minutes.

Axel wasn't in class when she got there. He was often late so she didn't start to worry until after the opening isometrics session.

"The crazy isn't here." Anita pointed at Axel's empty terminal.

"He's not crazy," Amy said as she wiped her forehead. It was very warm exercising in two suits of clothing.

"He's not *normal*."

"Maybe he's sick?" a boy named Alan said.

"How could they tell?" Anita laughed, but no one else did. The older girl's eyes narrowed and she looked more closely at Amy. "You're getting fat! Look at you! Is that why you get out of training dorm? Because your mother steals extra rations for you?"

"She doesn't!" Amy blushed, first with anger at Anita and then with self-consciousness as the other students stared at her. With two sets of clothes on and her pockets stuffed full, maybe she did look odd, but nobody had noticed until now. "Why don't you mind your own business, Anita?"

"The truth hurts!" the other girl taunted.

Amy turned her back and sat down. Giving Anita a good kick would be very satisfying, but it would also start a fight. Anita outweighed her by thirty pounds, and Amy was not stupid. Nor did she want to attract the camera's attention to herself this morning. She just wanted to get out of here.

She could go up to level twelve and try to find Axel, but if he had already left the shelter and was on his way here she'd never see him in the crowds. And if he was sick . . . she didn't want to go home again without even trying to get outside, but she didn't want to go without him.

The buzzer rasped for class. Talking ceased. Amy's first tape was called "City Living" and was a retarded form of citizenship. She had been given the same course for three years now, its scheduling part of the watcher's system to dull her mind as much as possible.

"Hallway traffic flows fine if we all keep in single line," the worn tape chanted. "Traffic never gets too tight if we all keep to the right," and "We will have a better day if we give sirens right of way."

No rhyme had been found for "Don't shove on ramps," or "Wasting water kills us all." While her screen showed a series of warning symbols, the voice track explained the meaning of these road signs for the illiterate. "Don't run," was a picture of a boy with broken legs.

Amy pretended to watch by staring at the top rim of her screen. Next to her, Anita's screen was showing the simplified steps of assembling thong sandals as part of the girl's career training. To the left, Ann was learning how to repair the sealing unit of a pipe extruder. Amy had seen both those tapes so often she knew them by heart.

Sometimes, if she allowed herself to think about how bored she was, a feeling of deep tiredness would come over her. Her body would seem to weigh a thousand pounds, her stomach would start to churn, and she would have to get up and go to the sanit to keep from fainting or throwing up. So she had learned not to think about it but instead would try to remember a story in the book and flash it on the screen within her mind.

This might be the last time she ever sat here like this. She knew she should feel bad about that, but she didn't. Her mother still talked about how bad she felt when she had to leave her learning center for training dorm. Amy wondered why; it wouldn't matter to her if she never saw Anita again, or Ann, who had once been her best friend until Anita warned her that Amy was a reader. Ann didn't even know what "reader" meant, but she had quit talking to Amy. Or Alan, who was very bright, but pretended to be a normal, and passed hours playing with himself until the watcher had him fixed. Or Agnes, who never spoke, just smiled sometimes.

At midbreak, when all the others went to get their lunch from the dispensers, Amy went to find Axel.

There was much less traffic now. Some places one could see all the way across the corridor and, at intersections, down the halls. Greasy fluid had been spilled on the up ramp to level ten. Maintenance workers were spreading lint to absorb the slippery oil. Amy waited at the edge of the crowd until the ramp was clear, then let the crowd precede her so she could take her time.

She liked walking ramps. They curved and she found curves pleasing in a world where everything ran in straight lines. For safety reasons, the ramps were well lit and kept fairly clean and, where they opened out onto a level, gave the only feeling of spaciousness she knew.

There was no need to ask directions; the youth shelters were in the same block on every level, at B and seven down. At the shelter two guards sat on stools just inside the sliding glass doors.

They were talking to each other, and while one looked up and saw her waiting, he ignored her. She waved, then pressed her nose against the glass, looking lost and scared. After a good five minutes one of the men bestirred himself enough to rise and open the door a crack, but he neither spoke nor looked directly at her.

"Thank you," she said, suspecting that if she let her anger show, he'd slam the door as if she didn't exist. Adults did that to kids, or anyone smaller than themselves. "I've come to get Axel 32281. He's a transfer in my class on nine, and he didn't show up. Is he sick?"

The man gave no indication of hearing her, then said, "Watcher want him?"

"What do you think?" Her question wasn't a lie. Another little pause and then the man turned to the terminal next to their stools. "What's the number?"

"Axel 32281."

He repeated the number to the terminal speaker. "Axel 32281 is in-house," the computer immediately answered, its voice markedly polite compared to the human's.

"He ain't gone out, kid," the guard said.

"Is he sick?"

"How should I know?"

"Well, can I go see him?"

The guard looked at his cohort. "She wants to see a kid here."

The other guard shrugged. "Why not? No skin off my neck. Let her in."

She slipped through the open crack in the door. "Where—"

"Bunk has his number on it." The second guard nodded at a passage behind him. "Down there."

She had not imagined there were so many homeless children and suddenly knew she was fortunate by comparison. The shelter was a maze of passages. Above the entrance to each were numbers starting with 100-00 to 200 and continuing as far as one could see in the distance. Inside each numbered dormitory, row on row of three-tired bunks filled the space from floor to ceiling. Walls, floors, bunks, and blankets were all pale green and grimy with use and age. The place smelled of urine and despair, all masked with disinfectant.

Amy stood at the door to the 300 room, not wanting to enter. The place was almost empty. Only a few bunks were occupied, one by a small boy who lay whimpering and thrashing restlessly. Across from him an older boy lay watching the child, his face impassive. Two girls came running down the aisle and brushed past her out the door. She guessed they were late for class. There was no way to avoid it; she went in.

The bunk with Axel's number appeared to have been made with him in it. A ragged green blanket covered the mattress from head to foot. Axel was the fetal-shaped lump beneath the blanket.

After calling his name and getting no answer, she gingerly lifted the blanket from the bulge she thought was his head. He peered up at her, his expression changing from fear at not knowing who his visitor was to a frown of surprise. There were circles and puffs around his eyes as if he'd been crying a long time.

"You sick?"

He shook his head.

"Why aren't you in class?"

He shrugged.

She reached over and felt his forehead; he had no fever but he flinched away from her touch.

"Let me alone! Get out of here!"

She pulled her hand back and held it as if she had been burned.

"If you aren't sick, why are you acting like this?" she asked. "I thought you said . . . we were going to start looking today . . . I got all ready to go . . ."

He put on his new earguards and pulled the blanket over his head again, shutting her out, and started to rock. She watched for a moment, feeling disappointed and sorry for herself because no one seemed to want her around, even this boy who had nothing else. And then she considered him.

"O.K.," she said, and yanked the blanket off him, and pushed up his earguard so he could hear her. "You can stay here forever if that's what you want. And if this is how you're going to live, crying and sleeping all the time, it won't make much difference to you when you die. But I'm going. Good-bye, Axel."

She was halfway down the aisle when she heard him yell, "That's not my real name!" The boy minding the sick child looked around at the shout. She stopped and turned but could not see Axel for bunks. She walked back, slowly, not eager for more rejection. He had rolled onto his stomach and was peering through the dimness. "That's not my real name," he said again when he caught sight of her.

"It will be so long as you're here." She stood by the end of his bunk.

He stared at her with his puffy eyes. "Are you really going to try?" She nodded. "Now? Today?" She nodded again. "What if you can't find a way out? What if people try to catch you? What if . . ." His fears rolled him over on his back and made his legs writhe. "I *did* try, you know! And if I fail again, then I'm trapped here for always." His whisper subsided into a whimper.

"Yes," she agreed. "So am I."

"But you're used to it. You don't know anything better."

Amy frowned. There was something wrong with his logic where she was concerned, but she was in no mood to analyze that now. "Are you coming or not?"

"You're going now?"

"I already wasted half a day because of you." She waited for his response. When he continued to stare at her she took a deep breath and turned to go.

"Wait! I'm coming."

A buzzer signaled the end of lunch break. Cameras scanned the aisles as the children straggled back to the solitary confinement of their terminals.

The watcher's mouth twitched with irritation as he noted two empty seats. Now the girl was absent as well as the boy. Was that coincidence?

"Profile Axel 32281," he told the computer. The boy's file was brief; the first entry, made less than a year before, was a level four medix report.

"Unidentified pre-adolescent male patient admitted in co-matose condition suffering from concussion, severe lacera-tions, contusions, abrasions, and four broken ribs. Severely depressed. No print ID on file. Assumed illegal birth in ser-vice levels."

The file noted the assignment of a temporary ID and the subject's transfer to the shelter on twelve and the learning center.

The watcher dialed the level twelve shelter on a routine check and was told Axel 32281 had left the area, "with the girl you sent to get him." The security film was replayed, and as Amy's face appeared, the watcher felt a warning twinge of unease. Their joint absence was not coincidental; two abnor-mals were truant together. Why?

Because the watcher had higher ambitions within the se-lect world of authority, he was more thorough and resource-ful than most of his ilk. He noted the ID number of the medic who had first treated 32281 and called him. The medic remembered the patient only vaguely.

"Very disturbed—traumatized by some sort of assault or trauma—his reality parameter was shaken."

"In what way?"

"He believed he lived outside."

"When?"

"Before he was admitted."

"Had he?"

The medic's face closed. The question was close to treason.

"I want to know," the watcher insisted, "was he physically different in any way? Any evidence of solar radiation?"

"The patient was psychotic," the medic insisted. "It's in the record."

"You never considered he was telling the truth?"

"Don't be—the patient was disturbed."

The medic's indignant face disappeared as the watcher flipped to another channel. Perhaps, the watcher thought, I'm overreacting to a case of simple truancy. Still, it would be smart to alert the hall monitors.

6

"I was thinking," Axel said as they walked down the hall together, "it might be a good idea to go up to the eightieth level first. If there are windows there, it'd be so high that it would be like looking down at a map." When she didn't say anything, he added, less confidently, "Maybe we would see the ground and see if there are any people outside. And where they got out."

What is a map? Amy wondered. This was the trouble doing things with other people. They always had ideas of their own. Not wrong ideas, but different, so that a thing that seemed simple and direct got all muddled and difficult. Maybe it would be better if she went her way and let him go his. But if she said that, he'd probably just look at her and then turn around and go back to his bed and curl up in a ball.

"What if there is no place like level eighty and we just waste time?"

"Then we'll know anyhow." His voice was almost pleading.

"What good—" She saw a familiar face across the hall and forgot what she was going to say.

"What's wrong? You don't like my idea?"

She shrugged, not sure. "That was the crazy—from my apartment block. What's he doing up here?"

Axel turned to look, but the man was lost in the crowd. "Probably just wandering around," he said. "They go all over. You want to go up to eighty?"

"O.K." She really didn't want to, but if that man had overheard them talking about finding a surface door and had been told to watch her, he would expect them to go down, not up. But if he was a watcher, why didn't he just stop them?

The up-ramp entrance was on corridor A. Most traffic was local, from one level to the next. To avoid the congestion around the exits, Axel and Amy stayed in the through lane against the outer wall.

While the ramps weren't steep, the grade was constant. By exit 16, Axel said, "It's funny. Usually I feel so tired I hate to get out of bed, but today I feel like I could walk forever and not get tired. I guess it's because I have someplace to go and somebody I like to go with." Amy trudged on until exit 20.

"Do your legs burn inside?" Axel was puffing.

She nodded, too breathless to talk. She'd never climbed more than two ramps at a time in her whole life.

"Can we rest?" he asked. She nodded again, more emphatically.

"Why didn't you say you were tired?" he asked.

"Because four levels down you said you weren't so I wasn't going to say I was."

"Oh. That's stupid."

"No it's not. Let's find someplace to sit down."

They found space on one of the benches in the center of a traffic island near the ramps. The benches were full of old people talking with friends or just sitting, watching the crowds go by. A crazy lay on the floor; people stepped over her. Another wild-eyed woman marched around, arguing with someone who wasn't there, poking the air with stiff jabs. Axel eyed them uneasily; Amy ignored them.

She reached into a pocket and pulled out a chunk of protomush, handed it to him, and got a second, smaller piece for herself. "Hide it in your hand," she warned. "If the crazies see it, they'll try to take it from you. They're worse than rats." With the back of her hand she brushed away the hair that clung to her damp forehead.

"Why are there so many?"

"Rats?"

"Crazies."

She shrugged. "I don't know—there didn't used to be—not when I was little. It's getting worse. But the city is old."

"What does that have to do with crazies? The city being old."

"I don't know." She had never questioned that pat answer to all problems. "That's what the authorities say when people complain—What do you expect? The city is old."

"That's stupid." Axel took a bite of the mush and chewed thoughtfully. "Or, as they would say here, 'normal.' They call everything stupid 'normal.' I'd sure hate to be normal here."

Amy was too polite to tell him there was little chance of that. But he did seem different now, more alive. Maybe it was because his cheeks were flushed from walking that his eyes looked bright.

"That crazy's coming over here—he's seen us eating."

"Cram the rest in your mouth!" said Amy, following her own advice. Axel did the same, and the two of them got up and moved out into the crowd again.

By mutual agreement they rested every fifth level after that. Aside from the numbers painted on the wall at each exit, it was impossible to tell one level from the next. All looked and smelled the same. All the people looked the same. Slowly, without realizing it, they both became discouraged, and exhausted from breathing too much foul air.

At level forty-eight the ramp went off at an odd angle and ended. Just like that, with no notice and no explanation. Where the next up ramp should be was an area that gradually curved into the down ramp.

"Garbage!" Amy swore. "There's no eightieth floor! It was all a dumb story to tell kids. We came all the way up here for nothing!" She felt like kicking something or crying or both. They stood looking one way, then another, bewildered.

"Maybe the next ramp goes up."

"Then why not here, too?"

He shrugged. "It was just an idea. We could go see? Or ask somebody?"

"We could go back down too. It's just about the same distance."

"You sure quit easy," he said.

"I don't!"

"You do! The first time something goes wrong, you're ready to quit. You could at least come with me and look."

"O.K.," she agreed grudgingly. "But I think it's a waste of time. We could've been outside by now maybe if we'd gone down instead of up."

"Or we could be running around in tunnels, not knowing which way to go—like I did every time before."

That caught her attention. "How many times have you tried to find your way out?"

"Six."

"Six? They caught you and brought you back every time?"

He nodded, shamefaced. "When I used my ID card to get food or asked someone questions, a guard would always get me right afterward and take me back to twelve."

"Why didn't they take you to Rehabilitation?"

"Because they . . . they think I'm crazy and Rehab wouldn't help. That's what I heard one say—it would just make one more crazy."

Amy thought that over and wondered if they'd be so lenient in her case. Still, if Axel knew he wouldn't be punished . . .

"Why didn't you ever come up here by yourself to look?"

"I didn't know there was supposed to be any place you could see out. Besides, I probably would have been scared to come alone."

"Oh." There was a pause. "I always was," she admitted, "and I always wanted to see eighty." She started toward the corridor. "Let's find a public sanit before we decide anything else."

The boy made a face. "Do we have to?"

"I have to."

"Oh . . . me too, if we're being honest."

The sanit was marked by its blue and white sign of dancing water, a sign far more inviting than the interior. Public sanits were dangerous places, and children were encouraged to avoid them. There was supposed to be a guard assigned to each room, but the guards were never there. A security camera scanned the area, but the camera was usually broken.

"Don't look at anybody and move fast," advised the citywise Amy as she eyed the disreputable-looking adults who lounged inside the door. "Pretend you have to throw up. That keeps 'em away. Do what I do." She put her hand over her mouth and began to run, making retching noises in her throat. Axel ran after her, noting how Amy deliberately bumped into people and gagged. Instinctively the adults jumped back or shoved the children toward the toilets until

Amy and Axel found two vacant cubicles and slammed the doors behind them.

"That was really smart," Axel said admiringly when they were back in the corridor again en route to the far ramp. "Where'd you learn that?"

"Anita—the big girl who sits across from me."

"Oh. I don't like her much."

"Don't worry about it." Amy suddenly grinned. "If we're lucky, we'll never see her again." Axel started to grin back at the thought, and then, to her surprise, his face twisted as if he were going to cry. "What's wrong?" she asked. He turned away so she couldn't see.

It took him a little while before he could answer. "Nothing . . . I just thought what it would mean—if we *had* to see her again. It would mean we're still trapped."

"If we have to go back, we'll just try again." She spoke more bravely than she felt.

A siren went off down a side hall. Amy's stomach cramped at the sound. Maybe they'd been seen? To clear the right-of-way, the traffic crushed together and came to a near halt until the bright yellow car passed. People craned their necks to see who or what was in the vehicle. All Amy and Axel could see were the backs and shoulders ahead of them. Both children mouth-breathed to lessen the stench of body odor. Axel stood with his hands over his earguards, his eyes squeezed shut. Amy waited in controlled panic and wondered if it was true that she was "trapped"—for if she was, then so was everyone else. Didn't they mind?

When the crowd started to move again, she tugged the boy's arm to wake him up and they continued on their way. Perhaps because they were tired now, the corridor seemed endless. After a time Amy thought to look at the hall numbers. The school tapes lied—every level was not the same.

There were seventy-two halls in her sector of level nine, and a ramp every twenty halls. The hall they were passing here was number ninety-six, and no ramp was in sight.

Axel hadn't noticed and she didn't say anything, wanting to figure out for herself how this could be. But she couldn't. And there was no one to ask without revealing her strangeness to the area and the fact that she didn't belong here. She would wait and see. Maybe this was the top level?

After hall 121 came the ramps. They were narrower and much steeper, and the pavement was lined with traction bars. There were wheel marks on the pavement, as if a lot of emergency vehicles went up and down here. The children, already tired, trudged upward, eyes on the ground, seeing little around them, earguards on, shut into their own determined little world.

Up one slope, around the curve, up the next slope, dodge around people, around the curve. Rest. The time for their evening meal came and went without their knowing it. Ramp traffic thinned as time and levels passed. From level sixty-five on up there were gates and turnstiles. ID cards were needed to leave the ramp. They did not want to use their ID cards and betray their presence so far from home, so they leaned against the wall to rest and then went on. There was almost no traffic now. Both were so tired they could hardly lift their feet. When they reached the exit to level seventy, they found no turnstiles there.

"We'd feel better if we could rest and eat," Amy said, and Axel nodded agreement, too tired to talk. They left the ramp and stopped in exhausted bewilderment.

7

There was no corridor here. There was nothing familiar. The off ramp led to a long hallway that turned sharply to the right. Before the turn, a sign on the rough gray wall read: *No Unauthorized Personnel Beyond This Point* in red letters. No one else had exited with them. They were alone in this place.

"What does that mean?" Axel was so breathless his question was almost a whisper. Amy pushed her earguards up to hear. Too tired to repeat himself, the boy pointed at the sign. She glanced at it but didn't answer. Instead she reached over and pushed up Axel's earguards.

"Listen!" she said in an awed whisper.

There was no noise, only a faint, hollow roar. There were no people. Instinctively moving closer together, the two stared at each other, seeking an explanation both lacked. In the silence, dread crept into Amy's empty stomach and ballooned up to crowd her heart until she could hear its frightened thumping in her ears. And the worst thing was, she didn't know why she was frightened.

They must have stood like that for five minutes, getting back their wind and resting, but above all, listening. No one came down the hall; no one came up the ramp. Finally Amy could bear it no longer; she tiptoed around the curve to see what was on this level. Some fifty feet ahead, the hallway widened out and ended in a wall enclosed behind a gate of heavy bars. There were two other signs down there. She couldn't read them from here.

"Ahhh. No wonder it's empty—it's a dead end," said Amy. It was more a whisper than a cry of disappointment, but Axel dropped as if his legs had turned to jelly. She grabbed his arm, but he slid away in a curled heap.

"Get up!" Amy whispered, thinking he was shutting out. "Get up! You can't do this! Not now!"

His eyes closed, and he did not answer. He looked so awful that in spite of her anger she knelt beside him. Her leg muscles trembled so her sandal heels clacked on the pavement. She sat down, took off her sandals, and put them close by her hand in case she had to grab them and run. "Axel? Are you sick? . . . Maybe you need food?"

He didn't respond. She bit her lip and then chewed on it thoughtfully. Maybe he wasn't . . . she reached over and put her hand against his stomach. His heart was beating as hard and fast as her own. She called his name again and then just sat there waiting for him to move. When he hadn't stirred in five minutes, she decided he was just worn out. It would be hard to live the way he did. She pushed herself back against the wall, stretched her legs, and looked around.

She had never seen such a deserted area. There weren't even crazies here—or roaches. But then there wasn't much for them to eat up here either, she decided. There were a couple of rat holes in the cement. Rats could chew through anything.

She became aware of pain and on investigation found she had ugly blisters on the soles of both her feet. The top of her feet were rubbed raw wherever a strap touched. It didn't pay to wash sandals, she decided; dirt made them softer.

"I'm going to eat," she announced in a whisper. "You want some?" When Axel didn't respond to that enticement, she crawled over and felt his heart again. He was breathing almost normally; his pulse had slowed and his color was better. She adjusted his earguards so they wouldn't dig into him and then returned to the wall.

She had nearly finished a whole mush cake when her head lopped to one side and she fell asleep with the remains of her food in her hand.

She had a bad dream in which she heard a man's footsteps coming from a distance—slow, tired footsteps that stopped beside her bunk. She knew the man was watching her, and she tried to run but her legs wouldn't move.

The rats wakened her. She felt them first, then opened her eyes groggily and saw a rat sitting on her thigh, feeding from the mush in her hand as a pet would feed, totally at ease. Something tickled her stomach; a rat had crawled halfway into her pocket and was trying to back out, carrying a mush cake in its jaws. A third was standing up against her leg, bright-eyed, whiskers twitching, looking as if it intended to help the one in her pocket.

They felt her muscles tense as she wakened; at her slightest move the last crumb was snatched from her hand. Panicking feet dug into her belly. The trio fled, claws scratching on the cement, naked tails half raised. One raced across Axel and succeeded where Amy had failed in trying to rouse him. No sooner had the three-pound creature bounced on and off his chest than Axel jumped to his feet from deep sleep, arms flailing so wildly that he staggered into the wall.

"It's just rats," Amy said, grateful that he didn't scream.

"Disgusting! Disgusting! Dis—" He stopped mid-word and stared, remembering where he was, then shook himself and slapped his clothes as if to drive away all vermin.

"You want some?" Amy calmly held out the piece of mush cake the fleeing rat had dropped. Axel hesitated, shivered all over, and then took the food, ignorant of its violation.

"How much of this stuff did you bring?" he asked. He was

shaking and trying hard to pretend he wasn't.

"Five pieces. We've got three left." She wiped her hands on her pants.

"Smart," he managed to say, still struggling with his nerves as he sat down again.

"Not too—or I wouldn't have gone to sleep with food on me." She sat there thinking about the rats. She had never seen a live rat at such close range, only as furtive streaks along walls. Rats were kind of pretty if you looked closely; they had soft fur and they were smart—there was no place a rat couldn't go if it wanted to. She was as smart as a rat . . . smarter, even.

"You want to go on up the ramp?" Axel asked when he was finished with his food and seemed to have regained hope.

"Sure. We came this far . . . but I don't think there's anything up there," Amy said slowly. "Nobody's been here since we came . . . not even footsteps." She looked at all the space around them. "If this place is empty, I wonder why the crazies don't know about it and sleep here. Crazies sleep in any empty space."

"Maybe they're afraid to . . . not that it's scary . . . but maybe . . ."

"Yeah." Amy knew what he meant. She slowly got to her feet. The pain from the blisters was so bad she nearly cried. The idea of stepping barefoot on the traction bars in the ramp was more than she wanted to face at the moment. "I'm going to see what those signs say down there," she said and set off, walking gingerly, wincing at each step. She looked back to see Axel limp a few steps, then kick off his sandals and carry them, as she carried hers.

The big faded sign behind the security gate read: EMERGENCY GATE—*Freight Traffic Only*—DANGER" in large letters, and below in smaller print, "MAX. CAP. 10,000 LB." There was no picture to explain.

As they stood there puzzling over this cryptic the floor began to quake and the lights flickered. At first Amy thought nothing of it except to be surprised the hour was so late. Then from behind the walls came a great groaning noise as if the city were in pain deep down inside. A strange warm little wind blew across their feet and ankles, strong enough to ruffle their pants legs. The nicest scent Amy had ever smelled filled the air.

"Oranges!" cried Axel. "It's oranges!"

"Sh! What's oranges?"

"That smell—I never saw an orange in here—" He dropped to the floor on his stomach, his face pressed against the gate bars. For a minute Amy thought he was shutting out again. She didn't blame him. For all the pretty smell, that sound was getting louder and closer and the floor was quaking more and more. She wanted to run and hide. Then came a streak of light, like a crack along the floor behind the security gate, and the sound seemed to go up into levels above them and then abruptly stopped.

Axel rolled over onto his back, his face aglow. "It's a freight bin! They go up inside shafts! There's an elevator system!"

She shook her head and turned away. He was a little psycho. Might as well read the sign on the side wall before they went back to the ramp. From up close it was apparent the sign was on a door, a hatch-like affair that fitted snugly into the wall with only a hairline crack to define its outline.

The sign read:

Important Notice to Service Personnel
In Compliance with City Health Codes, All Personnel

Utilizing Sublevel Emergency Entrance Must, Repeat
Must Immediately Upon Leaving Contaminated Area:

1. Remove and Place All Garments in Discard Bin.
2. Enter Decontamination Chamber.
3. Proceed to Medix Unit.
4. Submit to Prescribed Sanitizing and/or Medicare.
5. Don Sterile Garments.

Lock Release Mechanism Activated by Pressure Sensitive
Switches, First Letter, Each Line. Press In Reverse Se-
quence Only. Access Time Ten Seconds Only. NOTE:
In Time of Riot Alert, This Door Will Not Open.

Amy read the sign six times before she understood even
part of what it said. "If you couldn't read," she remarked in
all innocence, "you couldn't open this door if you had to."

"Maybe that's the idea." Axel's voice was hushed with
thinking. "Maybe this level doesn't want people entering who
can't read . . ."

"That's everybody," said Amy. "That doesn't make sense."

"But not us."

"But we're not supposed to be able to read, and the authorities can't read—" Amy stopped, remembering the first
sign, *"No Unauthorized Personnel . . ."* Who was that sign
intended to inform? She turned and looked at Axel and
thought she saw her own confusion reflected on his face.
None of this hall made any sense.

"Let's open the door," coaxed Axel. "It might lead to the
elevator."

"Do you think the door would work? What if alarms go
off?"

"What if they don't?"

"We could go on up the ramp to eighty and see what's up
there, then come back . . ."

"If it opens, maybe we can find a way into the freight system and ride out." Axel stuck out a foot. "I don't think I can climb ten more ramps. Can you? Be honest."

"If we went very slow . . ."

"Let's open the door."

"If we're caught, they'll put us in Rehab and we'll never get outside." Amy was not ready to give up her dream. "When the authorities were done with us, we might not even remember we wanted to go."

"Sh!" The boy touched her arm and pointed back down the hall. "Voices," he whispered, and both strained to hear.

Without further warning, a yellow-and-black-striped guard car rounded the curve and headed straight for them. Two guards were on the bench seat. Seated atop the cage behind them was a shabby man with matted hair. Amy knew him; he was the crazy from her passageway. Without really thinking she touched the first letter of each line, bottom to top, and almost idly wondered if a person could die of fear. The door cracked open.

The trio from the patrol car reached the door in time to hear its locks click shut. The guards pounded on the door and tried to force it open, without success. The crazy stood and watched.

"You should have taken them yourself," one guard yelled angrily at the man with matted hair. "They're small enough—you could have nabbed 'em. You got a sleeper. You didn't need to come back for us."

"They're little," the man said. "The drug might kill them."

"Not much lost if it did," the guard said sullenly. "They'll die now anyway."

"You never used to lose them, Tracker," the female guard

remarked as they returned to the car. "You not only don't get paid, but . . . we'll have to report you. This is the fifth time in two years you failed us. And this time they were *children*. Getting old?"

When the man didn't answer, she looked at him. He was staring into space, his sunken eyes quite empty and very sad.

"Yeah," he said finally. "Old. Old . . . the city's old . . ."

When the car pulled away he turned and stared back at that closed door until the curve of the ramp blocked it from view.

8

Their escape door had no sooner closed behind them than a pink light flashed on. The light was so bright and hot that in their fright they were more terrified and flattened themselves back against the wall. From without came the boom of the guards pounding on the door. The wall vibrated with the blows.

"They'll get in!"

"They won't!" Amy spoke with far more confidence than she felt. The last thing she needed now was for Axel to shut out. "If they could read they wouldn't be pounding, would they?"

"What is this place?"

"I don't know."

He risked a glance at her and then squeezed his eyes shut against the painful glare. "Do you think the light will burn us to death?"

"How should I know?"

"Want to go out in the hall again?"

"No!"

"O.K."

There was a crisp little click, the pink light went off, and normal lighting came on. "Vermin eradication complete. Please disrobe. Discard all garments and footwear. Proceed to sanit. Thank you." The voice came from a tiny speaker above them.

Blinking to clear the pink spots from her eyes, Amy could see no one but Axel. She looked for a camera and couldn't find one. Nor were there grilles or grates to conceal such a unit.

"They quit pounding," Axel announced. He was standing with his ear pressed against the door. When she didn't answer, he looked up. "What are you hunting?"

"A watcher—I can't find any."

"Really?" He almost smiled with relief. "Let me look."

They were in a smooth white chamber. Straight ahead was a door labeled "Decontamination." To the right were sanit modules. The left wall jutted out to form a bench. Behind the bench was a panel marked "Deposit Garments Here." Track lights were mounted in the ceiling. Their search revealed no camera.

"Probably a recording turns on when the hall door opens," Amy decided as she stepped down from the bench they'd used to investigate. "People who are used to coming in here wouldn't be scared by it."

Axel was pointing at the bench. Their footprints were clearly visible in the dust. "People don't come here often."

"They must have an easier way to get into this level," Amy said as she tried to open the door to one of the sanits. When she touched the latch panel, a bell chimed softly and the recording recited itself again and shut off.

"Vermin eradication complete. Please disrobe. Discard all garments and footwear. Proceed to sanit. Thank you."

"That says we have to undress!" Axel was indignant. "Do we have to?"

Amy had spent her whole life obeying seemingly omnipotent, disembodied voices issuing from speakers. She had learned their instructions had to be obeyed to the last detail. It did not pay to disobey. She went over and tried to open the decontamination door. Again, as soon as she touched the door, the recording clicked on. "Vermin eradication com—"

"We have to." She spoke over the voice. "It's computer controlled. If we don't follow its steps, it will never let us out of here." She saw Axel slump onto the bench and fold his arms across his chest.

"I'm not going out of here naked. I'm not—"

"O.K. Stay here. Wait for them to get in." She pointed toward the hall door. "I don't like it any more than you do, but I'm going to do it."

"It's not fair! I hate this place!" He took off his sandals and threw them at the disposal panel. As they cracked against its surface, the panel opened and the sandals disappeared.

"Getting mad won't help." Amy used her sleeve to wipe the dust from a place on the bench, took the mush cakes from her pockets and put them on the clean spot. She added her earguards, ID card, comb, and toothbrush. Her sandals went into the disposal first, then her shirts, followed by both pairs of pants. "Just do it and don't think about it," she told him as she limped naked to a sanit.

"What if we get out on the other side and they're waiting for us there?" Axel was beginning to rock as he sat on the bench. "We'll be naked. It's humiliating!"

She halted; she had no answer to that. If she let herself

think about it too long she would be tempted to emulate Axel, wrap her arms around herself, and rock. "What if they're not?" she said, and went into the module.

When she came out, Axel stared at her, then reluctantly began to undress. "If you can do it, I can," he said.

Behind the decontamination door was a shower chamber. "Place your feet on the white marks, please," the computer instructed. "Grip the hand bars firmly. Keep your eyes closed. Procedure time—three minutes. Thank you."

"What do I do with the stuff I'm holding?" Amy asked, but the computer only repeated its order. Not knowing what else to do, she put everything in a pile on the floor and assumed the requested stance. Immediately fine jets began to spray against her. It was tepid, sweet-smelling liquid that felt like foam on her face and body. It was very pleasant—until the open blisters on her feet began to burn. Tears of pain mingled with the medicated water running down her face.

When the shower ended and the door into medix opened, she found all her possessions gone, apparently flushed down the shower drain. She had never been without an ID; for the first time she felt truly naked, exposed, as she went out the door.

The medix room was familiar. She stretched out on the wheeled recliner and watched the myriad pieces of equipment swing into position. A needle painlessly punctured her left arm and withdrew a blood sample. Seconds later, another needle entered with a nutrient tube attached. A roller-like instrument was working on her sore feet.

The medical computer analyzed this body, determined it suffered from severe stress, and treated it accordingly. Amy never knew when the relaxant was given and she went to sleep.

She woke expecting to be in her own bunk and saw instead

yellow walls painted with a strange design and a door marked "Exit." She was in a room big enough to hold six recliners, but there were only two, her own and the one next to her where Axel slept. A soft white-and-gray-striped blanket covered her and she felt warm and comfortable. She yawned and shut her eyes, still too dopey to think much. Then, slowly, memory and fear returned and she sat up.

Axel was sleeping with his hands clasped upon his chest, his mouth slightly open, snoring quietly. Between their two recliners was a chute, like those at the depot, and in the chute's receiving tray were packages.

When she got out of bed to investigate the packages, a number of things happened. When she stood, her body interrupted a light beam and triggered the computer. "Good morning," a lulling voice said. "Today is June ninth. The time is ten-seventeen a.m. Please dress and exit at your earliest convenience. Thank you." As soon as the recording finished, the wall panel behind the recliner opened, a small motor whirred, and Amy's recliner rolled into the opening. She dropped to one knee and saw the recliner positioning itself under the medix equipment as the panel closed.

The blisters on her soles were still visible, but the pain was gone. The tops of her feet had healed, and she could stand without wincing.

Axel stirred at the voice, and Amy saw his mouth close and his eyes open, then close again. He looked different, she thought, much better, in fact. She stepped closer to stare down at him. She had never seen him clean. His hair, free of grime and oil, was a mass of shiny black curls. The injected nutrient and sleep made his skin glow. After months in the dimly lit city his eyelashes had grown long and thick. He was pretty without all that dirt!

Deciding to get dressed before he woke again, she opened

one of the packages in the tray. All the clothes were white! She had never seen anyone wear white and wasn't sure it was allowed. And the cloth was smooth. It would show dirt so fast . . . and yet a computer had supplied it. She puzzled over it for a time, then shrugged—there was nothing else to wear.

There were two pairs of pants, two shirts, and a pair of strange sandals, bright red, thin soled, and very soft. And what was the oddest thing, one pair of pants had no legs and one shirt had no sleeves. She put those on first and wore the other clothes over them.

"Where are we?" Axel whispered from his bed and startled her. She'd been so engrossed in dressing she had almost forgotten he was there. She turned to see him lying on his side, watching her.

"Where we were, I guess," she said. "We got new clothes. All our own stuff is gone. Earguards and everything."

He didn't say anything for a long time and then asked, "Are we prisoners here?"

"The computer said we could go when we wanted to."

"When?"

"When I got up."

"Oh." Axel rolled onto his back and stretched and yawned. He seemed in no hurry to leave this comfort. "Do you think this is the only way people can get into this level—by coming through this hospital?" he asked.

"I don't think it's a hospital. . . ." Amy looked around. It *did* look like a recovery room. But the idea didn't make sense.

"The blanket's dusty too." Axel was fingering the gray stripes. "It's been folded and stored a long time—and the—"

"I don't care." Amy was suddenly bored with wondering. Too much was strange. And all of it was frightening. "The only way we're going to learn anything is to go out that door and see how we can get up to level eighty—or find your freight bins. All this is just wasting time. Are you able to get up or not?"

He was ready in ten minutes.

The exit opened onto a narrow passage, completely bare and white except for a red arrow painted on the floor and a small wall sign that said, "Press for Taxi." The words were meaningless to them. There were faint noises in the distance, none familiar. There were no people sounds or sirens. They tiptoed out into the passage, following the arrow.

"Look!" Axel whispered, and pointed. As she stared, the door slid shut behind them. They had entered level seventy.

9

Ahead of them stretched a wide service aisle of white concrete, bordered as far as they could see by massive metal objects. Everything was color coded. There were enormous red tanks and yellow towers. Thick clusters of white pipes traveled overhead, like precisely racked strands of spaghetti. A-shaped blue things marched off to the left to mingle with a community of purple octahedrons. Massive columns supported a twenty-foot ceiling.

The colors were all faded. Rust streaks and peeling corrosion blisters hinted of prolonged neglect. Leak puddles mirroring the red tanks confirmed poor maintenance. But the level was more brightly lit than Amy had ever seen. There was dust but no filth or litter. There was no sign of rats or roaches or people.

The two of them stood looking, listening to the muffled throb of pumps and overtone of fans. From far in the distance came a constant high-frequency whine.

"Where are we?" Amy whispered. "What is this place?"

"It looks like level one, sort of. Only clean."

"Is it machinery that runs the city?"

"I guess so."

"Nobody's here." Amy hesitated, then walked out into the aisle and peered down an avenue of tanks. Her shoes made no sound on the hard floor. "Nobody's here."

"Looks like it, huh?" said Axel. "Let's find the freight shaft. It was to the right of the door we came in, so it should be near here. . . ."

But it wasn't. Where Axel thought the shaft should be was nothing but a blank wall. They passed aisle after aisle of equipment before turning back to their starting point.

"There's probably no freight door on this side because there's no one here," Amy said, trying to lessen his disappointment. "There has to be another way onto this level. We'll find it."

"We could follow the arrows," he said. "I just hoped we wouldn't have to walk so much."

"Are your blisters hurting?"

"Not yet—but I don't want them to. We have a long way to go."

Yes, Amy thought, all the way back down—if we can ever get there now. And we've got no food and no IDs. And we're wearing white. If we don't find the freight shaft . . . She took a deep breath. It wouldn't pay to worry, wouldn't change anything.

They followed the arrow down the aisle between the red tanks, skirting the puddles, puzzling silently over what they saw. The directional arrow was repeated every tenth tank. Thirty minutes passed and they were only halfway across the level.

It was the first time in her life that Amy had ever been in so large an area devoid of other humans. She felt exposed and dwarfed by this place. She kept looking back over her shoulder to see if they were being followed, but no one was ever there. Slowly she began to relax. No people meant no danger.

Axel broke the silence between them. "I was thinking—did you tell your mother you were going away?"

"Not . . . no." It seemed the easiest way to answer.

"Won't she be worried?"

"No." Not unless I come back, Amy thought.

"How do you know?" He sounded sad for her, and she resented that, yet liked it at the same time.

"I just know."

He frowned. "That's good, I guess, that she won't worry. I feel bad about my parents—I'll bet they were half crazy for a while. They probably think I'm dead by now."

"Do you know your father?" Amy was surprised.

"Sure—don't you?"

"I don't have one—not a person I know," she added hurriedly, seeing him frown again. "See, Valory had me just because it was a baby bonus year. All the girls who had babies got better jobs and got to move from dormitories to apartments. The authorities do that when people die off and they need new people to replace them. The next baby bonus will be two years from now—Anita said she was going to have one then. But she doesn't really want a baby—just the bonus. Like Valory."

"Nobody has babies any other time? Just when the authorities want them?" he asked, and when she nodded, "How do they do that? I mean, I know how people have babies, but—"

"Drugs, I guess," Amy said blithely. "That's how the authorities do most things. Like when the people start getting really mad about the filth? Or the food gets bad? The authorities drug the water to make everybody happy until the problem gets taken care of. Or people forget about it."

Axel shook his head in disgust. "I really hate this place."

A directional arrow curved left and they turned onto a side aisle. At aisle's end they could see a door, high as the ceiling and wide. But before reaching the door they came upon another sign. It was suspended from one of the support columns. Below it stood what looked like an ancient fire alarm post.

Amy read aloud:

> "Danger—Warning—Danger. All Drivers. Secondary Defense System. Before proceeding, deactivate Unwanted Personnel Defense Unit. Pull Lever A down. Wait for green light before proceeding. Failure to observe this order will trigger laser fire when exit opens."

"What does that mean?" Axel read the sign again to himself and then out loud.

"I think it means if we don't pull that lever down, lasers will burn us if we try to open the door."

"Why would they do a thing like that?"

"I don't know. . . ." She shivered, thinking of being burned. "But let's pull the lever down?"

Lever A moved slowly, as if it had been a long time since it was used. When it reached the bottom of its slot, the panel behind the lever turned green and more words became visible. "This Unit Will Rearm in Ten Minutes."

A rumbling sound made them turn. The big door was sliding open. On the other side was a wide ramp sloping up.

"It's a long way to that door—let's run!" Axel said and raced off. Amy followed, but favoring her blisters gave her a leg cramp and slowed her down to a limping jog. A green light glowed above the door. She kept her eyes fixed on that light—and tried not to think what she would do if Axel got inside and she did not. Or if Axel got inside and she arrived just in time to be hit by lasers. She saw Axel turn, look back at her, and call, "Come on!"

"I'm coming as fast as I can."

To her surprise, the boy slowed down and stopped.

"Why are you stopping? Run!"

"Come on!" he called again and circled back to meet her, caught her hand and tugged her after him.

"Let go!" She tried to pull free. "You can make it!"

Instead of answering, he speeded up and towed her after him.

When they reached the open door, there was no sign of danger. They jumped across the glide track and were some distance up the ramp when they heard the door start to close. They stopped and turned to watch. Axel let go her hand, and she stood rubbing the circulation back into her fingers as the big door eased shut. Then, from both sides of the ramp and from the ceiling above the center of the door, panels opened. The light gleamed off antipersonnel lasers, six per side and three overhead, all aimed at the ramp entrance.

"Do you think they really work?" Axel whispered. The whisper echoed in this empty enclosure.

"I don't know." Amy was panting. "The only people they'd kill are ones who opened the door without reading the—" She remembered the first door, and her eyes met his as sudden understanding came. "Signs," she concluded weakly. "They'd kill everybody from the lower levels . . . all levels are *not* the same . . . they don't want us to come up here. . . ."

A great unreasoning anger took over her mind. In that moment Amy wanted to go back down all those levels and kick every authority she had ever seen, smash every camera and terminal and vu-screen, and scream to people, "It's all lies! All lies!"

Axel was shaking her shoulders and saying, "Stop it! Stop it!" She realized then she was making funny strangled sounds in her throat and her breath was coming in short gasps. "Take a deep breath," she heard him say, and with effort she made her lungs obey. "Again." Not until the third breath did she notice Axel looked very scared.

"Why did I do that?" she asked him. "Why does it make me so mad?"

"I don't know," he said. "It makes me more sad than mad. When I first got here, I just wanted to go to sleep and never wake up and have to live here again . . . you O.K. now? We should get away from here."

She nodded, touched by his worry. "What did I do that scared you?" she wanted to know as they walked on up the ramp.

"Nothing—except you kept looking at the lasers, and your eyes got bigger and bigger, and you got pale and started to shake and make funny sounds. . . . I thought you were going crazy."

"Probably was. My head aches now . . . that's why they don't want us to read."

"Don't think about it now," Axel advised. "It'll make you mad again and nobody thinks good when they're mad. O.K.?"

"O.K.," she said; but she didn't mean it.

Like level seventy the ramp was empty. On the wall of the first curve they came to were the words "Sub-basement II."

The ramp curved up past a set of closed doors marked "Sub-basement I." "What does that mean?" asked Amy, pointing to the words.

"I don't know. It doesn't make sense up here," said Axel, and they gave the doors a wide berth in case they, too, were laser-protected.

As they continued on, Amy walked along in a muddle of confused thoughts, trying to understand what she was learning—without much success. Every now and then she would glance over at Axel. He walked up the slope with his hands clasped behind his back, shoulders leaning forward. Sometimes he would see her looking at him and almost smile. Maybe he would become her friend, she thought. She no longer hoped for a best friend, but just someone she liked who would continue to like her once he got to know her. Valory always said it didn't pay to count on people, and mostly she was right, Amy thought. But there had been Janet . . . and Axel had come back to help her run. . . .

A patch of brightness on the floor ahead distracted her. It wasn't normal light but came slanting down in dusty beams from some source hidden by the curving wall. She touched Axel's arm and pointed. "Is that laser light?"

When he saw it, he stopped still and stared, and then, without a word, began to run toward the brightness. She watched in horror as he entered the light and whirled, arms outstretched, a shining white dancer with red shoes. His face twisted as if in pain and she expected to see him fall dead. But he did not.

"It's the sun!" he cried out to her. "It's the sun! I thought I'd never see it again!" He whirled again and suddenly bent double and sank down on his knees, and as she ran to him she could hear him sobbing, "I want to go home! I want to go home!"

10

"What are you doing down there?" It was a woman's voice close by, non-hostile but curious. "Why are you crying?"

Both children froze for an instant, then Axel gave a muffled sniff and hurriedly rubbed his face dry. Amy tried but could see nothing up-ramp, because of the sun's glare.

"Did you fall and hurt yourself? Or are you lost?" the voice asked, and when it received no reply, scolded, "You children shouldn't be down here. This is a deserted area—and not all the nasty people live in the lower levels. We have some here as well."

Nasty. Amy stored that word away to consider later. The figure walking down the ramp toward them wore yellow; the color glowed as it approached the sun and the woman became visible. She was about Valory's age, but taller and better looking—clean—and she walked with a casual self-assurance that to Amy meant only one thing. The girl decided to get the worst over with. "Are you an authority?" she asked.

To her surprise, the woman laughed. "Only on some subjects," was the inexplicable reply. "Now how did you two get in here without anyone seeing you?" She waited and then interpreted their frightened silence in her own way. "Not going to tell me, are you?" She grinned. "I remember when I was your age and went exploring—if I was careful enough I could get in almost anywhere. I'll bet you're not going to tell me how you got out of class either, are you?"

Amy shook her head, bewildered. Of all the strange things they had experienced, this woman was one of the strangest.

"Cheer up," the woman said. "You don't have to look so scared. I won't tell on you." She bent, took Axel's hand and tugged him to his feet. "You're not very lost. The door you sneaked through is just up there, around the corner, safe and sound. I'll take you back." She held out her other hand to Amy.

Amy hesitated, then accepted the hand, afraid if she refused she'd hurt the woman's feelings and make her suspicious. Her legs felt wobbly, but she tried to walk as if she weren't scared and they had come down the ramp and not up. Does that mean I'm *nasty*? she wondered. The stranger's hand felt smooth and boneless, as if it had never worked at all.

"Where does the sun come from?" Amy asked as casually as she could.

The woman glanced up at the rays. "I don't know," she said. "Maybe a hole in the ceiling. This is still part of the old structure." The subject didn't seem to interest her too much.

The ramp appeared to end here. A giant door came into view. Their guide was leading them toward a small door cut into the base of the enclosure. Inside was a busy warehouse stacked high with containers, rack upon rack, stretching floor to ceiling in long rows. There were several people and a variety of robots working, sorting and loading items onto conveyor belts.

"You go out through that far door"—the woman freed their hands so she could indicate directions—"cross the loading dock, go up the little ramp—and there's the promenade. You can see it from here. The through-way and Eastgate will be to your left—"

"Will there be sun out there?" Axel spoke for the first time.

"Of course . . ." Her face clouded as she looked down at

the boy. "You poor child," she said. "You were badly frightened in there, weren't you? Why did you go in?"

"He'll be fine," Amy said quickly, wary of too much interest. "I'm going to take him home."

"Good." The woman smiled at her. "You might give him a whiff of anti-traum when you get there—and take some yourself. You both look pale. And do me a favor—don't sneak in here again to play? If you do we'll have to close the doors, and I'd hate that. The ventilation's terrible in here."

A noise at the loading dock distracted her.

Amy looked and saw a white vehicle with blue lights flashing from its roof. Two plump men in pretty green uniforms got out and came strolling in, calling, "Where's the ramp access door?"

"Back there." The woman pointed. "Anything wrong?"

"Probably just a computer malfunction," one guard answered. As they passed, Amy read the word "Security" on the arm badge of one of them. Axel tugged at her arm; he had seen it, too. "Let's go," he whispered. She needed no urging, and they tiptoed away.

"The door's open!" they heard a man's voice call as they crossed the loading dock. "Anybody come through here today?"

"Let's run!" Axel whispered.

"No!" Amy held him back. "That'll show we're scared! Walk."

"There's no cage in the car," Axel noted as they passed it. "Maybe they aren't guards."

"What does security mean?"

"Guards."

They had almost reached the street when the woman called after them, "Children!"

"Pretend we didn't hear her," whispered Amy, "but

don't run. If we run they'll know we're guilty."

"What are we guilty of?"

"Coming from the lower levels."

"Oh."

They came out of the loading dock and turned right to put a wall between themselves and the woman calling after them. They were so intent on getting out of her sight that they didn't really see where they had arrived until Axel chanced to look up and gave a strangled little grunt of surprise. "Sky!" They had walked into an enormous domed enclosure.

"It's level eighty!" Amy said. "It's better than the stories say!"

Across the street was a tree-lined promenade where flowers bloomed and extraordinary people walked—big, clean people dressed in clean, pastel-colored clothing. Beyond the promenade balconied structures rose seven levels high with windows on each level. Courtyards separated the buildings, and in those courtyards there were fountains. The angled dome-support ribs cast a webbed pattern over everything below. Beyond that metal web was blue sky.

They hurried across the promenade and through the park, dodged among a group of children dressed in white, went down what Amy called a corridor between two buildings, and entered a passage that led into an empty space where water spurted up and tumbled back into a round pool and leafy green things grew up from stone pots. The air in this place smelled almost as pretty as oranges—but different.

"I've got to rest," Amy panted. "My side hurts—and my feet."

Axel looked back. "I think we lost them."

"I don't think they followed us," Amy said. She leaned against a tubbed arborvitae and mopped her face; then, seeing the fountain, went to it, cupped her hand, and drank. "I looked back a bunch of times and didn't see them—"

"Maybe there's no place to get out and they figure they'll get us soon without running."

Amy gave him an irked look—if there was a scary way of looking at things Axel would think of it. "And maybe they're just too fat to run and decided we were what the woman in yellow thought we were," she said, keeping her voice low.

"That's kind of stupid if they did," he argued. "Don't they trust their computer? It must have recorded our coming onto level seventy. They have our fingerprints on file."

"But now that we're here, we look like everybody else," Amy said. "All the kids I saw wear white like us. And their haircuts are all different, so ours don't stand out."

That they were temporarily safe was enough at the moment. She was more interested in these new surroundings.

She studied the buildings around the courtyard. It wasn't at all what the stories about level eighty had led her to imagine. For one thing, it was nicer than any story, clean and quiet and bright. Almost too bright. Why did they need so much light? And this waste of running water! All levels were not the same—and if the people down below knew something this nice existed, they would be so mad they would come racing up here . . . there would be a riot. . . .

"In Time of Riot Alert, This Door Will Not Open," the sign on level seventy had said. She hadn't understood until now why it said that. If all the people down below came up here . . . She imagined this space they were resting in as it would be if full of people—the crowd, the noise, people in the pool.

"Amy, come over here," Axel called softly, and when she came, he pointed down a long hall where people walked. In the distance were more trees; beyond them was a stretch of blue. "That looks like a park . . . you don't know what that is, but I think we can see out from there—maybe all the way to the ground!"

It wasn't far to the trees. Amy had already noted that this level seemed smaller than any of the levels below. Almost tiny, in fact. And the oddest thing was, there were so few people. The people walked along in ones and twos, and there usually was space between them. And in the places called streets, there were little cars that weren't emergency cars but just hauled healthy people from one place to another.

"If you don't stop staring, people are going to know you don't belong here," Axel whispered. "Pretend you've seen it all before."

"But it's so . . ." She didn't have words to describe it. "Are you used to this? Is this what it's like outside?"

"Some of it—but I never saw a place like this," he admitted. "This is sort of what I expected the cities to be, but richer looking."

Then they were in the park, a place where people sat on benches under manicured trees, with flower beds and walkways winding around lily pools with goldfish swimming in them, and long stretches of green grass. Amy had never seen anything so beautiful, and she kept telling herself the reason her eyes were tearing was all because Axel kept digging his nails into her arm to remind her not to yell and point every time she saw something wonderful.

People sat in the sunshine, talking, taking their wonderful lives for granted. She was studying the people, envying them, when Axel's hand on her arm gripped so tightly she nearly cried out—then she saw what had excited him.

They had reached the far side of the park, where the clear dome touched the floor and revealed the outside. In the near distance could be seen other domes gleaming under the sun. Glass-sheathed walkways joined one to the next. Between the domes stretched not chasms seventy levels deep, but a surface of stony clay and rubble . . . not ten feet below the spot where the children stood.

"You know what?" Axel's whisper sounded strange, as if he were angry but too surprised to let the anger rule. "Do you know what?" he repeated.

"What?"

"This isn't the roof. This is the surface—all the rest of the city is underground. I thought it was, but everybody said I was crazy. And after a while I quit believing—"

"I don't believe it!" Amy said. "The city is so big that the roof would look like . . ."

"That's clay, Amy, *clay*—bare ground. Look out there—you can see where it slopes downhill. That's why everything's dark down below. Why there are no windows. Why nobody gets outside. You just believed what you were always told because you didn't know any better."

11

Without knowing she was doing it, Amy freed her arm from Axel's grip and stood alone, looking out at the ground and the domes beyond. Then, feeling somehow numb, she left him and went to sit on the nearest empty bench. Her eyes focused on a crack in the red brick sidewalk, but she was unaware of seeing that. She felt nothing but an odd euphoria, as if she'd just seen something horribly funny but didn't understand the joke. If anyone had spoken to her then, she might have begun to giggle helplessly, as if her mental computer had shorted out from overloading.

After a time, Axel came and sat beside her. She paid no attention to him until he folded forward and put his head between his knees. She noticed that and wondered why he was doing it.

"Do you feel faint, son?" A white-haired man in blue sat down next to the boy and held a gleaming vial beneath Axel's face. He was the oldest and the biggest person Amy had ever seen. "Breathe in," he ordered. "Good. Now you, young lady."

A sharp clean scent went up her nose and threatened to make her choke. She turned her head away, but the old man kept the tube beneath her nose. "It's anti-traum," he told her. "Nothing fancy. I use it a lot myself."

The gas blurred and softened thought; nothing seemed to matter quite so much. As she looked at the old man, he seemed as kind as the woman in yellow had been. And for as little reason. "What did you do that for?" she asked.

"For? You looked sick. What have you two been doing?"

"Looking at the outside."

He smiled as if she had said something funny. "No wonder." He capped the vial and tucked it in his shirt pocket. "Makes me a little sick to look at it, too. It's the everlasting sameness that gets to you. The trick is not to think about it."

The old man stood up. He was very tall, and as she looked up at him, Amy wondered how he could live on her level; he would be constantly bumping his head. He'd never fit the bunks. He returned her stare, and a quizzical expression appeared on his face.

"You two weren't thinking of trying to get outside? Were you?" When neither answered, he shook his head in disapproval. "So you were. People your age often do . . . should know better. There is no way out, you know. Even if there were, you'd die out there."

"That's not true!" said Axel.

"But it is, son." The man sat down beside Axel again and patiently tried to explain. "Granted the air is clear again, but if you could get out, where would you go? What would you do? The city stretches on forever. And there is nowhere to walk. Besides, what's the point—there's nothing out there."

"There is—beyond the city," Axel insisted.

The old man shook his head again, sadly this time. "There is no *beyond*, son. Domes like ours cover everything except the oceans. I'm old and I know. I've seen a lot in my time."

"But I live—" Axel caught his near mistake and altered what he was going to say. "But if everything is city, where does the food come from?"

"Why, from farms down below," the old man told him and gestured at the surface outside. "That's all farms under there. Floor after floor of nothing but hydroponic farms. They're all automated. Crops grow under lights and in the water from the rain. Rainwater collects and runs down the grates around the outer edges of the domes. Nothing is wasted. The sewage—" He regarded the two of them skeptically. "You should have been taught that by this time. Are you sure you weren't?"

"I never was," Amy said in all honesty. "Do you think there are people down there?"

"In the subsurface levels?" When she nodded, he chuckled. "You've been told those old horror stories too? I used to enjoy them when I was your age. About all the people who lived down below in darkness and gloom . . . they used to give me nightmares. I must have been fifteen before I quit believing they existed."

Amy and Axel exchanged glances. It was impossible to tell if this man believed what he was saying or if it was the kind of lie adults told children.

"Do you know . . ." Amy was being as careful as she

could be. "Did people *ever* live in the—what did you call them?—subsurface levels?"

"Apparently they did," the man said. "Long time ago. Before the domes were built. They thought it would be more energy efficient to live underground back when you couldn't breathe the air outside and the sun made people sick. But when things got better and the domes got built, the people who had to live down there protested. There were evidently some bloody battles . . . riots and all. But the authorities settled things."

"Who fought who?" Axel asked, and the old man shook his head.

"I don't know. Since history was removed from the learning centers, everyone's forgotten the old stuff. Happened before I was born. Long before you were born. Doesn't really matter. It's all past now and forgotten. Nobody lives that way any more. Everything's the same now."

The three sat in silence for a time, each lost in thought until Amy said, "I think we should go," and Axel reluctantly stood up.

"You youngsters have come a long way," their new friend said, rising too.

"How can you tell?" asked Amy. "Do we look different?"

He smiled, glad of the chance to display his years of wisdom. "Most people wouldn't notice it, of course—and it's not that you look much different. But your speech is different. I've learned, depending what group of domes people come from, they have their own way of talking. Like you two. Only the funny thing is, you both have different accents."

"Oh," said Amy, and resolved to talk as little as possible. "Well . . . good-bye.

"Does he really believe all that?" she asked when they were

safely out of the old man's sight. "About nobody living down below? And the farms and all?"

"We didn't know what was up here," Axel reminded her.

"No . . . just the stories . . . no one believes."

"Then it's not what he believes either but what he's been taught," Axel reasoned. "And if you're not taught the truth, you don't know. Like we didn't know we had to come all the way up here to reach the surface."

"But somebody knows—the woman at the ramp knew— the authorities know. . . ."

"Or else the guards wouldn't have shown up at the ramp," he agreed. "But they probably don't tell most of the people here. Just the ones who have to know."

"I wonder how they manage that?"

"The same way they keep people downstairs from finding out about this place probably."

Axel turned around and walked backward to see if they were being followed. Amy tried to emulate him and nearly fell over her own feet.

"How do you do that?" she asked, impressed.

"Easy." They were following the park rim of the dome, heading toward one of the glass tunnels connecting this dome to the next. "You tell your feet to walk backward, and you practice a lot—and after a while they do it!"

"Don't you bump into people?"

"You practice where there aren't any people."

"Oh." She couldn't imagine a place like that. "Do you think he's right about there being no way to get outside?" she asked. "Maybe we should find your freight shaft—at least that might connect with the freight belt—"

"It's got to be in that warehouse," he said. "But then we'd have to go down into the darkness again. . . ."

He seemed so upset by that idea that she felt sorry for him. "The old man's probably wrong anyhow," she said. "Like about the rest of the stuff he told us. He sounded like that man in the depot the day we got your earguards—the one who said we'd never see outside."

"But this man's nicer. I wasn't afraid he'd hit me."

"Maybe it's not that he's any nicer, just that he lives an easier life," Amy speculated.

They walked along in silence for a time. The people they passed paid no attention to them, and Amy gradually stopped glancing over her shoulder to see if they were being followed. Axel was preoccupied with watching the sky, as if he could never get enough of it.

"Eastgate." She read the neon word above the entrance to the passage. "That's a pretty name."

"East?" Axel said. "We want to go west."

"We do?"

"That's where I come from. East just takes me farther away."

"Oh." Amy's sense of direction was limited to right and left and up or down level. As far as she was concerned, they had found a perfectly good exit and Axel was being picky. "What's west?"

"That way." He pointed. "It's always opposite. Besides, you can tell by the sun. It rises in the east and goes down in the west."

"Oh." It made no sense to her yet, but she filed that rule away to mull over later.

"So let's cut through the park and see if we can find a glass tunnel like this on the other side of the dome."

Amy hesitated and then said, "O.K.," because it seemed to matter so much to him. "But let's go down to Eastgate first. Maybe there's a hall that connects with the other traffic—"

"Don't say 'hall' up here," he advised in a warning whisper. "Say 'street.' 'Hall' is something different here from what you—we think it is."

"Oh. How about 'corridor'?"

"Don't say that either."

"What else can't I say?" asked Amy, made uneasy by having something more to worry about and thinking she liked Axel better when he was less bossy.

"I don't know yet," he admitted. "We won't talk much."

"I was just talking to you—not strangers."

"Don't be mad. We have to think of those things."

Eastgate did empty into an avenue that cut through the park and stretched the width of the dome. They could see the opposite exit in the distance.

It was less than a fifteen-minute walk, but it seemed far to her once they left the trees behind. The higher the roof overhead the more exposed she felt and the more edgy. For the first time, she wondered if she really wanted to go outside, if she could get over this fear of openness. When she looked up and saw all that empty space, it made her want to find a safe hole somewhere and curl up . . . like Axel. . . .

"Are you hungry?" His questions interrupted her thoughts.

"Starving."

"Me, too. It's all this exercise."

"I wish we still had my mush cakes."

"I wish we had spareribs and beans and corn bread and coleslaw and noodles—"

"Is that all food?"

He nodded. "You'd like it, Amy. It's so good! When we get home, we'll get you all kinds of good things to eat." He grinned over at her. "It's going to be fun showing you all the things you've never had. You can live with us and—"

"Who's *us*?"

"My parents and brother and Ty and Margo's parents, Oki and Ben—they have a baby—"

"A real baby?" She hadn't seen a baby since she was three years old.

"Yeah—it's cute—and—it may not be a baby by now."

"Will they want me there? It costs a lot to keep a non-worker. Water costs. Food costs—" She was reciting her mother's litany to cover her fear that it was her own person who would be unwelcome.

"They'll want you," he assured her. "They'll be so glad to meet you!"

She gave him a weak smile, pretending to believe him, and changed the subject by pointing to a building they were passing. "That looks deserted," she said. And it did. Holes gaped where windows had been. The entrance was bricked up. A large crack ran from the base to halfway up the face of the structure.

"One fell down there." Axel pointed toward a pile of rubble where several people were working, stacking brick onto small, sturdy flatbed trucks.

"Maybe it shakes up here at night, too . . . but this doesn't look half as old as down level." She finished the remark in a careful whisper.

"A lot of down level is cut out of solid rock," Axel informed her. "It wasn't built so much as it was tunneled out. All the corner blocks are solid rock. So are the ramps."

From the center of the glass tunnel they could see in all directions. The old man's insistence that the city was endless looked true. Domes went all the way to the horizon. They were standing there looking when a klaxon began to honk somewhere down the way. All at once all the people walking in the tunnel veered over to the walls and stood, looking out. The klaxon stopped.

"It must be a warning of some kind," Amy whispered. "But what are they looking for?"

Axel squinted against the sun. "I can't see anything."

Amy sneaked a glance at the people closest to her; they were staring down at the ground. Two had their eyes closed. Maybe it was some kind of rest period.

The hiss of wheels on pavement made her turn. The biggest car she had ever seen was speeding through the tunnel. The car was silver, and under its bubble top rode a driver with two large people in the rear seat. The people were dressed in white with sparkly things around their necks.

"Oh!" a shocked voice beside her said; an arm reached out and pulled her against the wall. "Don't *look* at them! You know that's not allowed! What if they saw? Someone I knew once looked at them—you should know better!"

The car passed before Amy could see more, and she was very disappointed as well as scared. "I'm sorry," she told the woman.

"What were you thinking of, child? Suppose they stopped?"

"What would happen?" said Axel.

"You looked too—I saw you," the woman accused him. "Don't think that just because these two are more lenient than the last they aren't the same. And your youth won't help you if they decide to make an example of your disobedience."

The klaxon interrupted her berating, and when it stopped, she turned and almost ran away, as if not wanting to be seen associating with them.

"What was that all about?" Axel whispered as they walked on.

"I don't know—they must have been authorities in the car, but we never had to hide our faces—" Amy felt a stranger's arm encircle her shoulder; a hand closed upon her upper arm, and even as she tried to jerk away, the grip tightened to a trap.

"Don't make a scene," a woman's voice murmured above her. Amy tried to twist free and was held more tightly. Beside her, she saw Axel struggling with a tall young man who caught her frightened glance and said, "It's all right, Amy. The authorities want to meet you."

They knew her name, they were authorities—that could mean only one thing. They were caught and going to be sent back down below to Rehabilitation. They would make her "normal"—

She did what any self-respecting rat would do when cornered. She bit!

12

In her dream she was taking a test. The computer had three different voices. It asked odd questions, about her mother and Janet and the book. It flashed printed text on its screen and made her read the words aloud. And she couldn't lie or pretend she didn't know answers. She didn't even want to lie, but she knew she should. Sometimes the dream felt very real.

The computer told her to rest, and it asked Axel questions, and she could hear him answering. Then she knew it was really a dream because Axel never answered tests. Her tongue felt thick, and her mouth was very dry. A too-sweet taste filled her throat, and the dream faded into nothingness.

"Amy? Wake up. Please wake up!"

Axel's voice was coming from a long way off. A hand patted her arm, hesitated, and patted her again. "Amy?"

She didn't want to wake up; she couldn't remember why. She wanted to stay asleep. The hand patted her cheek, two awkward, gentle pats. "Amy?" He seemed to be pleading with her—but Axel should know it did not pay to wake in Rehab. She moaned and turned her face away from that hand, and then it slapped her.

"Amy! Wake up!" He yelled so loudly into her ear that her head jerked back and her eyes flew open—then shut against the overhead lights.

"You awake now?"

"Yes." The word slurred out through her dry lips.

"Here's some water. Open your eyes so you don't spill it." He picked up her right hand and folded it around a cup.

"Are we in Rehab?" She managed to get the words out.

"No. We're still up above. You can't taste the air, and I haven't seen any bugs in here."

Amy took a deep breath; he was right about the air. She opened her eyes wide enough to let her see to guide the cup to her mouth. The water was the best she'd ever tasted.

"They drugged us," Axel said. "You got more than me because you fought so much."

"How do you know?"

"I've been awake a long time. I learned—down there—not to fight them because they always drug you. . . ."

She finished the water and opened her eyes. She was in a small white room, and Axel was sitting across from her on the lap of a recliner.

"What is this place?"

He shrugged. "Don't know—a questioning room, I guess. There are two doors behind you. One's locked. The other's a lava—a sanit. There's a speaker in the wall. That window—

like thing there is a one-way mirror. We have glass like that at home—you can see out but no one can see in. It's nice—in a house."

"Is there more water?" she asked and started to sit up.

"I'll get it." Axel took the cup from her limp hand and walked around behind her into the sanit. When she turned her head to see where he was going, the room began to go around and around.

"I'm so dizzy."

"It goes away," he said as he came.out with more water. "It's the drug they gave us to make us answer questions—"

"What are they going to do to us?" she asked, still only partially alert. "I had the weirdest dreams . . . the computer was testing us . . ."

"They weren't dreams. And it wasn't a computer. They did give us tests. They asked us all kinds of questions." Axel pointed at the glass square. "They're probably still watching and listening to us—behind there."

Amy glanced at the brown-mirrored glass. She had spent her life being watched and knew there was nothing she could do about it. Whether the watcher was behind a glass panel or looking at a vu-screen made no difference to her. She never let them see how she thought or felt anyhow.

"You know what?" Axel said. "I think they believed me when I told them I came from outside."

"Why? What did they say?"

"Nothing . . . but when they said, 'Where were you born?' I said Mercer Medical Center, and they said, 'On what level were you born?' and I told them outside—and there wasn't any talking for a time. Then they started to ask me questions about home—how big was the settlement and where was it and who my parents were. And how did I get here. And they didn't talk for a while after each answer."

"But if they didn't talk . . ."

"I know . . . but I think they believed me. None of the people down level even asked any questions about home. They just said I was psycho and there was no place like that."

Amy thought that over as best she could in her half stupor. "Maybe they'll send you home," she said. "Maybe that's why we're here and not in Rehab yet." That thought was frightening. She looked to see how far it was to the sanit door from her recliner and decided to risk walking the six feet. It took effort to stand up.

The sanit was immense; she could stand in the middle of the room with her arms outstretched and not touch any wall. It was all so clean it sparkled, and there were no roaches. There was a dispenser which, when she pressed the labeled button, gave her a comb, a washcloth and towel, and a medicated toothbrush. Her mouth hurt when she brushed her teeth, and she remembered the woman hitting her when she bit.

"Can they see through that mirror in there too?" she asked when she came out again.

"Probably. If they want to. They can in the youth shelter's sanits."

She made a face. "I don't think I'd want that job."

The speaker in the wall made an odd coughing noise. The two children exchanged glances.

"They were still listening," Axel said and looked as if he'd like to shut out. The two sat silent, stricken with shyness.

The door next to the sanit slid open. The same young couple who had captured them stood there. He was carrying a large tray; she was carrying a gun, in her left hand. Her right arm was bandaged from wrist to elbow. Neither one looked at all friendly.

Without a word, the man set the tray on the floor, just far

enough inside so that the door would slide shut past it. He backed away. His partner kept the gun leveled on Amy and Axel. Neither child moved a muscle until the door had closed.

"They're afraid of us," Axel whispered, sliding off the recliner to go look at the tray. He seemed pleased by their captors' fear.

"Is that where I bit her—her bandage?"

"Yeah—" He grinned at Amy. "You did a good job!"

Amy didn't return the grin; she was wondering how bad the punishment would be for the crime of assaulting an authority.

"Oranges!" In his excitement Axel forgot they were being listened to. He held up a waxy orange-and-brown ball. "Real oranges! And bread and chicken—and carrots. It's all real food!" He picked up the tray and brought it over to the space between the recliners, then sat cross-legged on the floor beside it. "Come and eat."

He held an orange out to her. She took it, smelled it, and bit into it. It was the best thing she'd ever tasted even though the tart skin made her throat half close and she choked. Axel frowned. "I think you'll like it better if you peel it," he suggested and started to peel the other orange to show her how.

"What do you do with that part?" She pointed to the peel he was discarding.

"Throw it out."

"I'm not wasting any good stuff," she said firmly and took another bite.

"You'll get a stomachache," he warned. "Please don't eat it like that."

The meal became a lesson, with Axel as the teacher and Amy as the pupil. It wasn't until they were almost finished eating that it occurred to her. "This was a test too!" She glanced at the mirror and lowered her voice.

"What?" he whispered.

"The food—it was all *your* kind of food. None of it was like what we eat down below. I'll bet they gave us that on purpose . . . to see if you knew what it was. I didn't."

"But that's silly—they probably eat this stuff all the time. It's what we ship in—"

"But *we* don't eat it—not on level nine or anyplace else down there. And if you'd been born in the city, you wouldn't know what that food was any more than me."

"But what if they don't have your kind of food up here?" said Axel.

"Why not? We eat it . . ."

"It's not very good." Axel was being kind. "You wouldn't eat it if you had something else."

Amy chewed awhile in silence. "I wonder why we don't," she said finally.

"I think it all comes up here."

"Congratulations!" The voice came from the speaker so unexpectedly that both children jumped. Axel bumped the tray, and carrots made orange stripes on the white tile floor. "Would you mind rising, please? The committee would like to see you."

13

Axel quickly struggled to his feet and turned to face the mirror. But Amy failed to obey. Perhaps it was the drug they'd given her so liberally; she didn't feel like standing and saw no reason why she should. It wouldn't pay; whatever the authorities were going to do they'd do anyhow. She wasn't going to cooperate and make it easy for them.

"Don't be afraid," the man's voice assured them. "We will not harm you. Stand and face the window, Amy."

Amy took a bite of fried chicken, another of butter bread, and chewed the mixture with deliberate pleasure.

"You'd better get up, Amy," Axel whispered. "Don't make 'em mad."

"I'm going to finish eating," she said. "I may not get the chance again. They've had hours to stare at us through that window. Why interrupt us now—except to show us they can? We're not real to them, you know. We're just something they watch on a vu-screen."

"Amy!" Axel was frightened.

"You're wrong, Amy," the speaker said. "You are real to us. Too real. You are the first to completely breach our security precautions in five years. You are welcome—if only as a warning that we are growing lax."

"Welcome to what?" she asked.

"Why, to . . . you have a very literal mind."

"Are you the authorities?"

"That's what you call us."

"Are you going to send us back to be rehabilitated?"

"No."

"I don't believe you."

"That is of little consequence," the voice informed her. "I admit that we did consider returning you, but decided in your case it would be pointless. Your kind exists to supply us with the goods and services we need. To be effective, rehabilitation would result in two more nonproductive consumers— useless eaters. We have enough of those already."

Amy didn't understand much beyond the fact that the

authorities said they were not going to be sent back. "What are you going to do to us?" she asked, putting down a drumstick bone polished clean.

"Your phrasing implies we are insensitive. Since you are both intelligent—"

"Will you let us go? Let us go on outside like we want to? Let Axel go home? We only—"

A snort of irritation interrupted Amy. A second man spoke, but not to her. "This is a waste of time! We've learned all we need to from them. You will eventually realize, Chairman, that I am right. Intelligence at their level is no advantage. Nor is it amusing. It is simply a burden to them and trouble to us. Disposal is our best means of security."

There was an interval during which several muffled voices argued, and then Amy heard the Chairman say, "You may leave, Radnor."

"They'll never belong! Not up here or down there!" The voice called Radnor was angry. "They won't belong and they won't forget—or forgive. They look harmless now because they're children. But they will grow up and become revolutionaries. You cannot afford to make exceptions, Chairman—you've never served sublevel. I spent five years down there among those sullen animals! One hint of weakness and they'll turn—"

The wall speaker woofed with feedback and went off. Axel waited a minute and then sat down on the end of the recliner. "I wonder who he was," he said.

"Somebody who doesn't like us," Amy said calmly as she gathered up the carrot sticks from the floor. "Do you want this—" She had to remember the name. "Carrots?" And when he shook his head, she ate them.

"How can you do that?" he said, watching her.

"The floor's clean."

"No—I mean, how can you eat now? That man just said he thought we should be disposed of. Don't you know what that means? They let us hear that on purpose. They could have turned him off."

Amy nodded, thinking. She munched for a time, like a meditative rabbit, then said innocently, "I wonder why they don't like us so much. Not just us, but people where we come from. The woman on the ramp said people down below were 'nasty,' and Radnor said 'animals'—like we were rats. People hate rats . . . people are afraid of rats . . ." She stared up at the window as if lost in thought. "Maybe they're afraid of us—the people in the levels under them?"

Axel started to grin at that idea. "Oh, sure!" he said and then thought about it. "Maybe . . ."

"They're probably still watching us, huh?" Amy pointed a carrot stick at the window.

"Probably."

"I'd like to see what they look like."

"I'd like to get out of here." Axel got up and began to pace about the little room with the purposeless energy of a caged thing. "I don't care what they look like. We finally find the surface and I can see the sun, and then they pen us up in this box. . . ."

An hour passed and seemed like four, and then without warning the door opened. A young man stood there, arms folded on his chest, one shoulder resting against the frame. He was dressed as they were—in white—but his shoes were black and he wore a wide black sash belt with a handgun tucked into it. He was short and muscular with wide, blunt hands, like the paws of a badger. He looked first at Amy, then Axel. Amy returned stare for stare. He had pale green eyes. She'd never seen green eyes before. She brushed the crumbs off, stood up, and went over for a closer look.

"You're not going to bite me, are you?" he asked, but he didn't seem worried by the possibility. What was better, for an adult he didn't seem hostile, not even a little bit.

"No . . . not unless you grab me." She stopped more than arm's length from him.

"I won't touch you," he promised. "Unless you try to run. Then I'll have to kill you."

"Are those your real eyes?"

"Yes. . . ."

"They're pretty."

"Thank you." He pushed himself erect with a slight thrust of his shoulder. "My name is Elton. I'm your guard. Please come with me."

"Where are we going?"

"It doesn't matter," Axel said quickly. "So long as we get out of here."

Elton led them out into a deserted hallway and onto the street. The park was nowhere in sight. Amy stopped and turned to look back at the block they had come out of. It looked like all the other structures around.

"What is this place?" she asked.

"The security center."

"Are we in the same dome where they caught us?"

"No."

She waited for him to say more, and when he didn't she commented, "There aren't many people here."

"No. This way, please," he said and pointed to a small blue van-like car parked nearby. "Open the door, please, Axel. Take the rear seat. Now you, Amy."

"Where are we going?" Amy asked again.

Elton hesitated, then said, "No place bad. Get in."

They were no more than seated when a clear panel rose to separate passengers from driver. The children exchanged worried glances and then resigned themselves to the fact that they were in this level's equivalent of a cage. Elton eased himself into the driver's seat and the car began to move.

The sensation of being carried in a wheeled vehicle was novel to Amy. She wasn't frightened by it, but it made her feel helpless, as if she were a thing with no will.

"You'll get to like it," Axel assured her, but she wasn't convinced. The drug was wearing off and depression was setting in.

There were round windows on either side of the seat. As they looked out, the city did seem endless, one dome much like the next, as dull in its own neat way as the lower levels. Elton drove on and on, not talking, going always in the same direction. The motion of riding began to make Amy feel queasy, and she closed her eyes.

"At least we're going west," she heard Axel say as she drifted into a doze. "The sun's setting."

The light outside was as dim as the lower levels when she woke up. The car was still moving. Axel was glued to his window. Elton slumped in the driver's seat as if he were tired. There were a lot of people on the streets, and the windows in the tiered blocks were yellow with light. The dome roof was more visible now, reflecting back the lights beneath.

"What made it get darker?"

"It's night," Axel said. "The sun went down."

She knew she was supposed to understand that, but she didn't. In her world, "day" and "night" defined time, not light level.

"A lot of buildings have fallen down." Axel pointed out his window. "Like that one." She leaned over to see, but they had already passed. "It's been like that the last ten domes or so . . . the people still look the same—well fed, big and clean—but when we go through the glass tunnels, you can see domes over across that don't have any lights on."

Amy puzzled over that. "If they got the shaking up here at night, that might shake things to pieces? The city's old . . ."

Axel shook his head. "This part's much newer than where we came from—see, there's a big one!" He leaned back so she could see where an entire section of the dome's interior structure had fallen to ruin. Walls thrust up at odd angles and ramps reached up to end in mid-air. Barricades lined the street. Even that portion of the park and promenade was gone. The area was deserted.

"Do you think he'll tell us what happened here?" Axel pointed at the driver.

"Not the truth. Authorities never answer questions. They just talk until you get tired of listening and give up."

If their driver heard this exchange, he gave no sign of it, and when they fell silent again, the only sound in the van was the steady hiss of wheels on the pavement. The fewer people in the dome, the less traffic, the faster he drove. Amy closed her eyes and listened; she could tell each time they left a dome and entered a glass tunnel by the increased roar in the smaller enclosure. They were in a dome when the van stopped. Elton got out. "Wait here," he said.

The van roof shut off their forward view. From Axel's window they saw the guard walk over to a small square building and disappear inside. The area was so quiet they could hear his footsteps echo. Something began to make a metallic screeching sound.

"What is that?" Amy whispered.

"It sounds like a metal roll-up door," Axel said. "Maybe they're taking us inside that building, but I can't see it opening anywhere."

That made no sense to Amy. She peered out the window on her side and saw the dome wall curving up over a stretch of bedraggled park. Standing water reflected lights from somewhere. The place looked deserted.

"Where do you think we are?" she asked.

"I don't know."

Long minutes passed, and they waited. Elton didn't come back. An hour passed. They tried to talk to fill the time and keep from worrying. Neither could think of much to say. Elton still didn't come back. Amy curled up on the seat, closed her eyes, and listened to Axel fidgeting. Finally his movements stopped, and then the sound of his breathing told her he had fallen asleep.

"Amy?" The whisper in her ear tickled and she reached up to scratch. "Amy, wake up." Harsh gray light flooded her eyes as she opened them and made her squint against the glare. Her neck hurt from sleeping at a funny angle. "It's dawn. The guard didn't come back." She turned her head and found herself nose to nose with Axel. "He's gone. I can't see anyone around here—anywhere."

She was too groggy to think. "You mean he just left us? Locked in here?"

"The van door's unlocked."

She stared at him.

"Come on, Amy, wake up!" Axel shook her shoulder. "We've got to get out of here while we can!"

"Yeah, O.K." She sat up. "You're sure—"

"Come on!" He slid off the seat and out the van door to the pavement.

"Wait!" She reached out and caught his arm, then crawled out to stand beside him. "Maybe it's a trick. Maybe they want us to try to escape so they can shoot us. Where there's nobody to see—"

"They could have done that last night. Why wait till now? Come on!"

"Shhh . . ." She heard another sound, a strange chirping noise. "What's that?"

"Sparrows. They're inside the dome. That means there has to be an opening somewhere."

"Sparrows?"

"Birds."

She vaguely remembered the word from Janet's book—and a picture of a pretty pink-and-white thing called a cockatoo. She remembered how funny that word had sounded to her then. But birds lived outside . . . "How did they get in here?"

"That's what I'm trying to tell you," he said impatiently, "they got in from outside somewhere. Come on. Let's look!"

Amy hesitated. The van door's being unlocked was no accident, she was sure of that. Elton, or somebody, wanted them to get out. But for what purpose? And where was he now?

"There!" Axel's triumphant whisper made her jump. "It *was* a roll-up door I heard!" He punched her arm in jubilation. "Look!"

Where the glass tunnel to the next dome should have been, she saw a dark oblong of ribbed metal that looked like an afterthought, a makeshift construction to close a hole. Except not all the hole was closed. At the bottom of the oblong was an opening.

"Let's go!" Axel whispered more urgently.

Still she hesitated, until he yanked her arm and pulled her into a run toward the door. She didn't try to break free, but she did expect at any moment to hear a warning shout, or the high-pitched whine of a laser—or something. This was much too neat, too easy. Something was wrong. Maybe the authorities wanted to give them the hope of escape and then catch them again to prove there was no hope. Like the reinforcement tapes in the learning centers.

14

They pushed their way out into a thicket. Where the glass tunnel should have been, only part of its framework remained. The glass lay in shards on the ruined roadway. Through the ground fog that blanketed the city, they saw the dome across the way, once connected by this tunnel, was also sealed shut by a metal door. There were no lights in that dome either.

Amy was trying to look at everything, trying to understand, but it was difficult to think and run through this tangle of green stuff at the same time. Everything was wet. Her shoes, pants legs, and shoulders almost immediately felt damp and cold and made her shiver. Glass crunched beneath their feet.

Axel pointed. "If we go around that dome that way, it leads toward home," he whispered.

"How do you know?"

"We came out the Westgate door. Besides, we have to get off this glass. If anybody's awake and listening, they can hear us walking here."

She looked back. No one was following them, at least no one she could see. She turned and ducked away from a tree branch Axel brushed past. The leaves whipped and showered her with drops and a sprinkling of aphids. They're probably watching us go, she decided, but there was no point in saying it aloud and scaring him. She brushed the bugs away, and they smashed into green streaks on her sleeves and fingers. She made a face; outside bugs weren't sturdy. You'd have to really stomp a roach to make it squish like that.

· "How come all this green stuff is growing here and not around the first dome we saw?"

"Maybe better soil—or less heat exhaust from empty domes."

"What are those scratch noises?"

"Insects—singing."

She hadn't known insects sang. She made a mental note: smash easy—sing funny songs.

"Are these plants like the ones inside?"

"That's sumac"—he pointed—"ailanthus, burdock, ragweed . . . mostly weeds and scrap trees."

"Why scrap?"

"Things people have no use for. Like weeds, they just grow where they can. Don't ask so many questions."

That nonhuman, living things could be classified as to their usefulness and acceptability was a novel idea to her. She mulled it over and wondered if plants, like people, were called good and bad and what plants did that qualified them for those labels.

When they had walked far enough around the second dome to see ahead, they discovered there was only thicket beyond. Both tunnels and dome on the south side were missing, and on the north only the skeletal frame remained. By standing on tiptoe and peering up over the thicket, they could see the domes behind them and the tops of three more farther to the south. But there were none ahead.

"Maybe the ground goes downhill." Axel hurried on.

Amy had to have downhill explained, and when she understood, disagreed. "I don't think so. I think everybody lied again.. The city does have an end. I think Elton brought us out to the edge."

"But why?"

She shrugged. "Who knows?"

Axel stopped so quickly that she ran into him and knocked him to his knees in the grass. "I'm sorry."

He looked up at her, his dark eyes bright with an idea. "What if they want us to escape? To get away? They said they didn't want to send us to Rehab. And they can't just send us back down level because we've seen too much and we can read—we can get back—"

"They could kill us," Amy said. "Real easy. Just one injection. One laser shot."

"Maybe they're too nice to do that. We're children . . ."

Amy wasted no thought on the possibility of authorities being "nice." "And if we went back to level nine and told people what we've seen up here, do you know what they'd say? 'Sure, kid.' " She pointed her right index finger at her head and made a circular motion to indicate madness. "They'd think we were crazy—especially you and me. They might believe Anita—she's normal."

Axel wasn't listening. "I keep thinking how the questions changed when I said I came from the greenbelt . . . like it worried them as much as surprised them. Maybe my parents have been looking for me and were told I wasn't here. Now the authorities find out I am . . . was . . . and decide to let me go home."

"Why not just send you back? Don't the authorities know the way to where you live? Don't they come to check on things?"

"No. They used to—long ago before my father was born. But they always got the flu when they came. So they quit. Everything's handled by computer. The authorities now might not know any more about us than I knew about them before. They might not even know *how* to send me back. They don't seem to know much—I mean, look at this." His disgusted gesture took in the ruined domes. "They let this all fall to pieces."

The intelligence implied by preventive maintenance had little meaning to Amy. To her the city was old and "old" things were discarded as quickly as she ignored that theory of Axel's. "O.K., if they want to let you go," she said, "but why me?"

"But we're *together*," he said in all innocence. "We told them that when they questioned us. They wouldn't send me one place and you another. That wouldn't be fair."

Amy searched his face and saw he believed that. While she was grateful to know he thought of her as a friend and was touched by his naïve faith in the authorities' respect for fairness, she didn't share his belief. "Maybe we'll understand it after we walk awhile," she said, and held out a hand to help him up. "You're going to get full of bugs if you sit there too long."

They pushed on to where the next dome had stood and found the foundation still there, the rubble almost buried under vines and briers and sumac. The sites of five more domes lay in a westward line, each one more obscured than the last, until not even glass pebbles showed beneath the ground cover. When the sun finally broke through the fog in midmorning, the children were several miles from their starting point and the city was visible only as shining mounds on the eastern horizon.

"Where are we now?" Amy asked as they stood resting and looking back.

"I don't know. Somewhere." Axel scratched a mosquito bite on his arm and grinned at her. "Outside—that's all that matters. I haven't felt this good since right before I fell into the freight bin. Do you have anything in your pockets to eat?" He spoke as if it didn't matter much.

"No. Do you?"

"No."

"Are you hungry?" Amy asked.

"Kind of. You?"

"Not yet."

"Good."

"Is it far to your place?"

"I think so . . . a couple days' walk at least. We can probably find water. . . ."

By two o'clock Amy was hot and dirty, tired and hungry. Her legs had been repeatedly brier-scratched, and she itched from sweat and mosquito bites. Outside was very different from what she had thought it was going to be. In the old book there had been pictures—she remembered a beautiful one called "Autumn in New Hampshire," and another of big black-and-white animals on a green field; beneath it the mystifying words, "Minnesota is a dairy state." Without realizing it, she had expected to step out into an orderly, captioned picture. Instead she was in the reality of this outside. And she wasn't sure she liked it.

The landscape was full of gullies now, eroded yellow clay scars that slashed across their path, some so deep that climbing down was difficult and getting back up the other side was harder.

"I've got to rest," she said, and sat down on the sandy bottom of one of the gullies.

"Not in the sun," Axel said. "You can rest up there in the shade."

"I thought you liked the sun."

"I do—but it'll burn us. We're not used to it any more." He looked closely at her nose and forehead. "You've never been in it before. You'll burn worse than me . . ."

"It doesn't feel *burning* hot. Just sweating hot."

"Just trust me?" he pleaded. "You know all about the city and helped me—but I know more about out here. And the sun can burn—so slow you don't notice it until you hurt."

"Does it hurt bad?"

He nodded gravely. "Your eyelids get all puffy and close. You get water blisters all over and feel stiff, and you throw up and—"

She scrambled up the cliff-like gully wall to its top, climbed over on her hands and knees and pushed herself erect. As she turned to watch Axel's progress behind her, something moved in the left corner of her vision. She turned to look, but it was gone, whatever it was. There was only green and clay in all directions. Her eyes watered from the glare.

"What is it?" Axel was panting beside her.

"I thought I saw something—back there."

He shaded his eyes with his hands, binocular-style, and scanned the area to the east. "Nothing but a flock of crows," he reported.

"Birds?" She shook her head, and then, seeing the worry on his face, decided to keep her fear to herself.

"You want to rest here?"

Resting didn't seem like a good idea any more. "Not now. Later."

They went on across land that looked as if, sometime long ago, man had leveled every tree and hill, covered it all with garbage, and then covered it all again with clay. Where the gullies cracked open the flat surface, ancient plastic bottles, glass, and dull metallic shapes protruded from the clay. Along some gully bottoms rain had washed mounds of refuse into crevices. Amy would always pause to look at these collections and wonder at them.

"Where did it all come from?"

"People used to live here."

"Where did they go?"

"Who knows? People have lived all over—everywhere."

She didn't know where "everywhere" was. "You mean . . . here, on the top—or underneath?"

"I didn't know about underneath," he said. "There too, I guess. But all over the top of the earth."

"Who lives out here now?"

"Doesn't look like anybody—" He had glanced back to answer her, and he paused in mid-sentence, staring into the distance.

"Did you see a man there?"

"I don't know." He was whispering again. "I thought I did, but . . ."

"Was it Elton?"

"He was wearing brown, and skinny—"

"Let's hide someplace and rest and see if anybody shows up."

"O.K."

They crept into a thicket so snarled that the branches hardly left them room to huddle. There they sat, arms wrapped about their folded knees. A few minutes passed; the flies and mosquitoes found them and droned about their ears.

"Crush. Don't slap," Axel advised. "The sound of a slap travels. And don't rustle."

After a few attempts at crushing, Amy decided it didn't pay and tried to ignore the bites.

"There's another good thing about roaches," she whispered. "They don't bite."

"You can have 'em," he decided. "What you saw—did it look like Elton?"

"It was white. I just saw a flash, sort of, in the sun, and then it was gone behind the green stuff."

"Maybe there's more than one—you don't think they'd take us back now?"

"Sure they would. If they didn't want us to get away," she said, and saw Axel rest his head against his folded arms, eyes closed as if suddenly exhausted. She was sorry she had been so honest, but the words were said now.

It seemed as good a time as any to rest. She hadn't realized how tired she was until she sat down. She closed her eyes and found that felt better. The sun was hard on eyes accustomed to the forty-watt brightness of level nine. The throbbing in her head diminished. Other sounds grew more distinct. Insects and birds were singing; the leaves were rustling in the breeze. Where her nose touched her bare arm, she could smell the lingering perfume of soap.

She sniffed the alien scent and wondered at this small detail of luxury. The dome people lived so differently . . . and yet Axel hadn't seemed surprised by any of it. He was different now; he hadn't shut out ever since he saw the sunlight on the ramp, she remembered. And while she was glad, still it worried her. It was as if the closer he got to the outside, the more he remembered the person he used to be, someone she never knew. Maybe, if they got to his place, he would change into a very different person, and maybe he wouldn't like her any more. Maybe he would think she was nasty—or stupid. Or maybe he wouldn't want her with him because she reminded him of a lot of bad things.

"Would you like him back the way he was, scared and crying? Would that make you feel safer?" her conscious asked her, and she had to answer no, because she knew instinctively that that had been a form of death for him. And yet she was afraid, for all her life the people she had cared about had turned away from her. Except Janet, and she had died. It didn't pay to count too much on people.

A stick cracked somewhere across the gully, and her head snapped up. Beside her Axel slept, his mouth slightly open in exhaustion. She peeked out, trying to see through the leaves.

A tall, thin man in city-issued brown was walking along the other side of the gully, one hand above his eyes to shield them from the sun. The other hand clutched the knot of a cloth bag he carried slung over his back. There was something familiar about his face and walk. If it weren't for his short hair . . . she imagined him with longer hair, and dirty, and then she knew him. It was the crazy who used to sleep in her hall.

15

How did *he* get out here? She was so surprised to see him she almost asked the question aloud.

He stopped across from their hiding place and stood staring down into the gully, shaking his head and muttering. Even at this distance she could see his eyes were bloodshot, and she wondered if they hurt, like hers. She watched him shift his bag from one shoulder to the other and slowly walk on south, following the gully until the bushes hid him from view.

Mosquitoes dotted her ankles. She was just about to scratch when something white moved out of the greenery and Elton came into view. At least it looked like Elton's body; the face was hidden by dark goggles and a white hat. He missed their hiding place by fifty yards and disappeared in the same direction the other man had taken.

Amy sat frowning and scratching; were the men together, or was each hunting them for his own purpose? It was all very confusing. She forced herself to wait until the pursuers could get far ahead, and then she touched Axel's arm to wake him. They set off again, deeper into the brush.

The way would have been hard for an experienced hiker, properly dressed and shod. The surface ranged from clay to mud to a scree of glass and plastic shards. The smallest hills were cut deep by erosion, and there were pits where landfill had settled. Thorned creeper vines with waxy green leaves grew in morbid lushness, as did a more delicate-leafed plant whose brown vines cut like wire.

The children's shoes, glove-soft for indoor wear, were scuffed and cut. Thorns tore their sleeves and pants legs, and scratched hands and legs already welted from mosquito and fly bites.

"How can you live out here?" Amy was trudging after Axel along a deep sand gully, batting away at gnats that swarmed around her head.

"It's not like this where I live," he said. "Not like this at all. I don't know what they did here, but it must have been something terrible."

"Do you think there's fewer insects out of this ditch?"

"Sure, but those men can see us up there."

"That's true." She smashed a mosquito on her pants leg, and blood mingled with the dust. "How long do you think it'll take us to get out of here?"

"The badlands, you mean?"

"Well, to where outside is nicer?"

"Today and most of tomorrow. You see up there?" He pointed ahead. "Those are hills—or maybe mountains graded down. After we cross those we should be out of this stuff."

Amy peered into the distance and felt a sense of dread; it was *so far*. And that was only part of the way they had to go. The sun's glare hurt her eyes, and she turned away.

"Why are you looking back?" Axel said, worried. "Are you sorry we came?"

She didn't answer right away; she was thinking that he didn't really know what was on the other side of the hills; he'd never been there—he was only guessing. At the speed they were going, it would take a long time, and they had no food. Which meant they might die if it took too long. But if they had to go back to the city now—at least it was clean out here and the air smelled good. . . . "No," she said.

In midafternoon they found a puddle. The water tasted muddy but no worse than the water Amy always drank. When they had had their fill and washed their hands and faces to ease the itch of insect bites, they sat and rested, too tried to talk.

In the stillness two robins came to drink and bathe with vigorous wing splashings. Avian generations had passed here without the presence of humans; the birds had forgotten old fears. A brown rabbit hopped out of the undergrowth and froze, nose twitching, to study the intruders, then hopped over for a few quick laps of water. A sparrow lit nearby, and the rabbit chased it away. Amy watched in silence, delighted by the strange creatures.

"That's only the second rabbit I ever saw," Axel whispered when the rabbit left. "They're not allowed in the greenbelt—they eat too many vegetables."

"They understand the rules?" Amy asked, and Axel giggled. She'd never heard him laugh before. It was a nice burbly sound.

"It's fenced," he said, and then frowned. "I forgot about the fence. . . ."

"What's a fence?"

His explanation lasted through their rest period and for

several miles thereafter, for everything he said was new to her and had to be explained.

"How high is the fence?" Amy asked after thinking over what he'd told her.

"About twice as high as a grown man."

"And you get hurt if you touch it?"

"Yes."

"You do all that to keep out soft little rabbit animals?"

He looked at her. "Yeah . . . it seems too much, huh? I never thought about it before. It was always called the rabbit fence. The authorities built it long ago."

"How will we get past it?" she wondered.

"There are gates," he said, refusing to be discouraged. "If we got this far, we can find a dumb gate."

As they walked, the land around them subtly changed. Vines gave way to grasses, ailanthus and sumac to spindly pines. Without realizing it, they stopped hearing glass shards crunch beneath their feet. Insects became fewer and less pesky, and there were fewer birds.

The sunset prompted a whole new series of questions from Amy. When she vaguely understood the situation, she asked, "You mean we're out here with no lights?" and Axel laughed again. "It's not funny," she said. "You're blind when there are no lights. It's very scary."

"But that's underground. It never gets that dark out here. There are the stars—"

Twilight and the uphill slope slowed their already none-too-speedy progress. When Axel found a cluster of pines half buried by creepers to form a natural lean-to, he decided they would sleep there.

Amy lay staring up at the vines and pine branches, finding comfort in the leafy ceiling. Something, insect or bird, was singing among the trees. Faint rustling noises came from the needles beneath her head.

After a few minutes Axel said, "I'll be right back," and sat up and crawled out. "We're going too far north," he announced when he returned. "From the position of the stars, it looks like it's June."

"Oh." She didn't understand a word of that . . . except, "That's what the computer said when we were in the medix chamber—something about June ninth." She yawned widely.

"I didn't hear that." The leaves rustled as he stretched out again.

"You were still sleeping. Should we take off our sandals? I never slept with sandals on."

"They're shoes—and our feet will get cold." He pillowed his arms beneath his head and considered. "So I was right. The sun is setting toward the northwest, and if we—I've been gone a year!"

One minute she could hear him talking and the next she was asleep. She wakened sometime during the night, frightened by the darkness and frightened to find another person cuddling next to her in the dark; then she remembered. There were little spots of light way up high above the trees. She stared at them until they danced, and then her tired eyes fell shut.

Birdsong wakened her. She lay listening, marveling that such little things could make such loud noises. The sky was light blue in the direction of the city. From here the tops of domes were still visible as beads of light along the horizon. A star glowed in the northeast. She was so hungry her stomach hurt.

"Do you think Elton and the crazy brought food with

them?" she asked Axel later, when they were walking again. "You think they know the way to your place?"

"If they did, they wouldn't be dumb enough to walk." His tone suggested he was not in the best of moods this morning. Amy retreated into silence.

Between them and the western horizon stretched nothing but hills, sugar pines, poverty grass, and bare patches of red clay. There were few hiding places for them or their hunters. Amy scanned the landscape for any spot that moved. None did, and she wondered if both men had given up and gone home.

The sun was overhead when they found the second water hole. They were up among those flattened hills, following a wide swath of valley that curved with engineered precision.

Axel began to run. She watched him stop long enough to take off his shoes before he pushed his way through the tall grass at the water's edge, splashed out into the center of the pool, and waved for her to join him.

She followed hesitantly, not sure she liked the feel of wet mud between her toes. The water felt cold and funny, creeping up her legs; then it buoyed her body up and threatened to tip her off-balance. She'd never been in deep water before, and she found it frightening, another thing too new to be trusted without learning more about it. But the pond did dissolve the dust of walking and take the sting out of her bites and scratches.

Tired of playing in it before Axel was, she waded back to shore and looked for her shoes. They weren't where she thought she'd left them. She looked around, recognized the path she had made on her way into the water, and set off in that direction. Preoccupied with keeping her eyes focused on that path, she didn't see what was hidden in the grass.

The thing she fell over was large and cushion-soft and made a sighing sound when her knee sank into it. She pulled her hands out of the marsh grass, brushed pollen from her eyes, got up awkwardly, and turned to see what had tripped her.

"I'm sorry!" The words were an automatic response, an instant apology for hurting the man who lay there. And then she looked more closely.

"Amy? What's wrong?" When she didn't answer, Axel called again, "What did you find?" and began to splash his way toward her.

16

It was Elton. His eyes, fully dilated, looked dull green-black in the sun. His lips had parted to reveal his perfect teeth. A shiny brown beetle was stumbling through the whisker stubble on his cheek. One arm lay folded on his chest; the other, dislodged by Amy's fall, was flung aside, palm open.

"I think he's dead," Amy whispered, watching the beetle's progress as if hypnotized. "He doesn't move at all."

Axel swallowed but said nothing.

"His hat's gone, and his clothes, his gun, and those things he was wearing to protect his eyes. . . ." She inventoried these diminutions of Elton's status, convinced that no one willingly parted with precious possessions. "But his shoes are still there. That's odd."

The beetle had progressed to Elton's upper lip. Amy knelt and flicked the bug away into the high grass. Axel gagged. She peered up at him, shielding her eyes against the sun.

"I've never seen a dead person before," he said apologetically. "Have you?"

"I don't know. I've seen lots of people lying on the pavement, but I was never sure if they were dead or high or sleeping. And I never waited to find out."

"Do you think the crazy killed him?"

Amy looked at the body again. "He doesn't look hurt—not from the front. His hair looks bloody—see? There in the back?"

"Don't turn him over, please."

"I wasn't going to." She stood up and shivered, although it was warm in the sun.

"Should we just leave him here?" Axel sounded a little shocked.

Amy nodded, surprised by the question. What else could they do? Besides, "Someone took his stuff," she reminded the boy. "That means someone knows he's here."

"Maybe he lost his hat and things walking. Maybe he got sick from the sun and threw them away to get cool."

"I don't think so. . . ." Amy took Axel's hand and tugged him away from the body. "Let's find our shoes and get away from here."

Axel was very quiet for the rest of the day. Amy wasn't sure if he was mad at her or thinking about Elton being dead, or if he was just tired and hungry, as she was. She wasted little thought on the dead man; he had been an authority, an enemy. Now they didn't have to worry about him any more. What they had to worry about was whoever killed him. It was that simple.

Late in the afternoon Axel found a patch of strawberries. Not the tiny wild variety, but descendants of plants once domesticated, their seeds bird-scattered. Birds had found these plants, too. Many of the berries were pecked and partly eaten. Amy quickly learned the damaged fruit was the sweetest. Her respect for birds went up a notch.

The berries were delicious and satisfied some of the hunger pangs. But even that didn't seem to cheer up Axel. Finally she asked him what was wrong.

"Nothing."

"Why aren't you talking?"

He went on eating berries, one by one.

"He was so quiet." The boy stared down at the red berries glowing in his hand. "So still . . ."

"Don't think about it," Amy said. "You want him alive again—and following us?"

"No. . . ." He took a deep breath and exhaled slowly. "But he didn't hit us or treat us bad. Maybe he was a good person."

Amy said nothing, wondering if failure to inflict physical abuse qualified a person as good. She could think of a lot of people who had never hit her but whom she had never once thought of as good.

"He probably only did what he was told to do," Axel went on in the face of her silence.

Amy shook her head; Axel was a little weird. It probably came from growing up outside and not having to understand how people acted in the city. "I don't think that makes him *good*," she said slowly. "Machines do what you want them to do if you press the right buttons. That doesn't make them good. That just means they'll do what they were programmed to do—like Elton."

"Don't you have any feelings?" Axel's question was an accusation. "Doesn't anything bother you? Even somebody dying?"

"It depends on who's dead," she said carefully. "If you're

talking about Elton, he said if we ran he would kill us—remember? I don't think he followed us out here because he cared about us."

"But he didn't hurt us. And he could have. And now he's all alone back there. Maybe his parents will wonder why he doesn't come home—"

"He's not *you*!" she said, thinking she understood his moodiness.

"I didn't mean that. Don't be stupid!"

"I'm not! You're imagining yourself lying dead in the grass. You're feeling sorry for yourself—not Elton. Besides, you don't even know if he has parents."

"Somebody must care!"

She wasn't sure if he meant care about himself or Elton. He looked angrily at her. "I don't want to argue about him, Axel," she said. "It won't change anything except to make things harder for us because we'll be mad at each other."

"Don't you even want to talk about it?"

"No. Not any more."

They sat a few minutes in uncomfortable silence, and then Axel said, "I saw a dead dog once with eyes like that, all glazed and the pupils all open."

Amy stared at the tri-leafed berry plant and saw Elton's face again. "Did you?" she said, and swallowed hard.

"Yes. It looks different on a person."

They spent the night under a tree, chilled by dew and wind. Both of them had stomachaches from the acidic fruit. Axel lay curled up in a ball, and when he slept he cried and talked in his sleep in the same voice in which she had once heard him singing. She dreamed of Elton's face and the beetle and some great dark terror overhead that woke her with ragged breathing and left her afraid to go to sleep again. She spent the rest of the night sitting with her back against the pine trunk, finding comfort in its solidity.

That day and the next were much the same. They walked on doggedly, existing on water and a few berries. Their feet were cut and swollen; all their muscles ached. Exhaustion was making them stupid. Amy's eyelids were badly swollen, and she was almost blind from sunburn. She trudged along, head down, all her energy concentrated on keeping on her feet, moving toward her goal.

Hunger made Axel remember all his favorite dishes: noodles and coleslaw, mashed potatos and ham. Amy had no idea what he was talking about and could not be tortured by imagination. She didn't feel hungry any more. In fact she didn't feel much of anything so long as they kept moving. She resented every stop. Stopping meant giving the blisters and cuts a chance to dry or scab, and starting out again was harder each time. It might have been less painful to walk barefoot. Surely the swelling would have been reduced. But there was always the risk that stepping on glass would totally disable them.

They walked over land once forested for centuries. Farming had destroyed the trees; cities had destroyed the farms; time had destroyed the cities. The land remained, slowly covering its degradation with new plant life. For many miles in all directions, they were the only humans, save one.

17

They had crawled in to sleep beneath the shelter of an ancient concrete ledge, the remnants of a roadway that once curved about a hill. Below them the outlet of a storm sewer had crumbled back to the creek it had been before man interfered. The creek meandered downhill through a stand of sugar pines and briers.

Amy heard a squelching sound and then felt a cool wet cloth being laid across her eyes. Axel could be so nice, she thought—he must have torn a piece off his shirt to get the cloth. ". . .s-sank you." Sun-cracked lips made speech difficult.

Water from the cloth dribbled down her cheek and into her ears. She reached up to scratch and her arm collided with a leg. The leg was too big to be Axel's. With a quick breath of fright she smelled sweat. She tried to move her legs; her ankles were tied together. Her heart began to beat too fast. Like an animal when it first senses mortal danger, she went still, her elbow still touching the leg.

"What is it?" She heard Axel's voice, next to her. Pebbles grated as he moved. "Amy?" His fingers touched her hand in reassurance. "Something's tangled on my feet," he said. "Must have been too tired to notice when— What's that smell?"

"Not me," she managed to say. "Someone's here." Axel let go her hand and struggled to get up. She pushed the cloth aside and winced at the glare through her eyelids. While she had slept, her eyelids had swollen shut. The leg shifted and moved away, and a hoarse voice spoke.

"Don't be afraid. You must not run. You must rest."

By pressing both hands against her face and peeking through the finger slits, she managed to make out a brown shirt and then the face of the crazy. She wanted to cry; it had all been for nothing.

"Is-s not fair!" Her cry of protest was slurred by the stiffness of her swollen face. "Why did you let us go—let us get this far—if you were going to bring us back? That's cruel!"

When he didn't answer, she decided he wasn't going to. Her eyes burned and she closed them and covered them tightly with the cloth. It didn't matter anyway, she thought; it had been stupid of her to hope. Stupid-stupid-stupid!

She felt the vines around her ankles pull tight, then break and she was freed. Dry leaves and pebbles rustled as Axel was untied.

"Sorry . . . ." The man spoke as if he had to stop and remember most words. "I didn't follow—I wasn't . . . I followed, yes—to the door on seventy. Most go down. You went up and I was glad. . . ." He lapsed into brief silence. "I could have stopped you. They were going to report me. I knew they would someday. I got ready. I climbed the old steps. Walked the old halls. Not even rats go there. People die. People forget old things . . . the city's old."

Amy shivered, not because he sounded crazy but because he sounded sane and much too sad.

"I saw you yesterday—moving in the distance. I was glad. They exiled you—not killed you there. I followed you again. But not to catch. To help. To make up."

"For what?" Axel said suspiciously.

"I watched her—the girl—and others, yes."

"Me?" Amy said. "Why?"

"You read. Others read. Nests of troublemakers. Like rats. So the authorities think. They are never sure. I was a reader. They found me out. Sent me to be retrained. But they let me keep my mind. Because I had the disease. I could recognize the symptoms in others. I watched for them. And reported. And lived."

"Did you kill Elton?" Axel asked.

"Elton?"

"You have his stuff."

"The dead boy by the water . . ."

"How did he get dead?" Axel persisted.

The man paused and then said, "I don't know. He was dead. He didn't need anything more. I did. I took it."

"You didn't kill him?" asked Amy.

"No."

Amy was not sure if she believed him, but Elton wasn't her chief interest. "If you don't want to take us back, why did you tie us up?"

"You would see me and run. So I tied you. So you would rest." She heard him moving around, dragging something through the grass. "You need food," he said. "You'll never get to the boy's people."

"You heard me talking to Amy?"

"Always," was all the man said.

He gave them what tasted like uncooked protomush, a small clump of something sour-sweet and rubbery. Both ate it with no questions asked and accepted the water he gave them in a handle-less mug.

"Do you have much food?" Axel's stomach was growling audibly over the protomush.

"You've had enough for now."

"If you weren't chasing us, where were you going?" Amy wanted to know.

"Anywhere. Away."

"You work for the authorities—why didn't you just go up to the domes?"

"Everyone works for the authorities." He hesitated. "Some they send down and never let back up again. But they don't tell you it's forever. They let you guess, slowly. To punish. And when you ask, they lie—to give you hope, to keep you working. Until all you want is . . . to die . . . to escape the dark city. . . ."

His voice trailed off into silence. Amy waited but he didn't say anything more. He hadn't moved; she could hear him breathing and she could smell him.

"Did he fall asleep?" Axel whispered.

"I'll look." Amy pushed an eyelid up far enough to peek out. The man sat staring straight at Axel. She dropped the eyelid back in place and moved closer to Axel.

"I'm sorry," the man said. "I scare you. It's been so long since I talked to people . . . I don't know how to act."

"Could you talk to other crazies?" Axel said tactlessly.

"No. They scared me," the man admitted. "I kept away from them—I'm not crazy, you know." He paused as if thinking that over. "I don't think I am . . . I wasn't. . . . Maybe you become what people expect you to be."

Amy heard him get up and then felt his hand on her ankle. She jerked her leg away. "What are you doing?"

"Going to take off your shoes. Let your feet heal."

"I'll never get them back on—"

"You will—when the swelling goes down."

"Let him, Amy," Axel said. "It's O.K. If he meant to hurt us he could have bashed in our heads with a rock before we woke up."

"But if we can't get our shoes on, we can't walk."

"We can't now," Axel reminded her. "I can't see much better than you."

"That's true," she agreed.

The man removed their shoes. Her feet did feel better then. He went away and came back with water and a rag and washed them, and they felt better still. The sun reached their resting place, and the man helped the children move back into the shade and made them comfortable again. Amy remembered she had never feared him when he slept in the passageway.

While he nursed them, he talked. At first slowly, haltingly, but as he got more practice, the words came easier.

"You've been all over the city," Axel said. "How far does it stretch?"

"Underground? Along the ocean. Inland. Far. I don't know how far. There are walls. Contamination barriers. Fire barriers. Structural walls. There was no plan. It grew—like mold in the dark. They enclosed and roofed. To escape the heat and cold and dirt. Their waste buried them sometimes. There was hunger. The authorities came back up. They built the domes—sealed off the city."

"Is there city under us now?"

"Could be. Some parts are dead. Empty. The domes are dying, too. I saw them. Not from sickness. From not knowing enough. Authorities fear people knowing. Only the ones they chose. So they can control."

"Who told you this stuff?" Amy asked.

"I was born above. In the dome. My parents were authorities. Long ago. There was fighting. They died. All their party died except the very young. We were sent down."

"Where? Who taught you to read?"

"Me. In the garbage mines. That's what I was. When I was normal. A miner . . ." His voice became more reflective as he remembered that time in his life. "We found books down there. Such pretty books. Below the veins of plastic and the metal and the glass. They couldn't watch us all. The watchers were afraid in the tunnels. The roof falls in sometimes. Buries people. And there's gas. Danger! Waste kills. . . ."

He rambled on, his voice becoming more and more weary as he talked, from either fatigue or depression at remembering. Amy listened, understanding only part of what he told them. He had apparently hidden some of the books he found and taught himself to read. Later he learned that other people wanted books; he had sold some and traded others for food and clothing. One of his buyers was a watcher.

Is that how Janet got her book? Amy wondered. Was it bought from a garbage miner—perhaps this man? She forced her eyes open again.

"Did you know an old woman named Janet?" She interrupted his monologue. "She lived in my room—"

"I didn't tell them," he said quickly. "They thought she was normal. Until she died with her book. She knew my name. She called me James."

18

"Who's Janet?" Axel was feeling left out of the conversation.

Amy didn't answer, so James explained, "She lived with the girl. Taught her to read."

"Was she a watcher?"

"No. A medic in the mines. She came when the gas was bad. Or the tunnel fell in. She got crushed. They let her care for babies after that. It was baby time."

"Oh," said Axel. "Now she's dead?"

The crazy hesitated and then jerked his head. "Yes." Axel looked over at Amy, who sat huddled, her hands over her eyes. "You never told me about her," the boy said, idly curious.

"No," she said, and hoped he wouldn't ask more questions. She didn't want to talk about it. There was no reason for Axel to care, and somehow, when you told something that mattered very much to you to people who didn't care, their disinterest spoiled things—made them cheap.

"You sleep now." Pebbles crunched as James stood up.

"I'm going to get branches. To keep the sun off you."

They heard him moving about in the grass, heard branches breaking, rustling noises, and smelled pine. After a time Amy stretched out again and tried to get comfortable. She slept and woke to darkness and lay wiggling her toes. She felt better. Her toes moved separately again—her feet had been swollen lumps. Soon she'd be able to run. She tried opening her eyes. Either it was dark or they wouldn't open at all.

"You awake?" Axel whispered.

"Yes."

"The crazy's gone."

Disappointment mingled with relief. She *knew* she shouldn't trust him! "Did you see him go?"

"I was sleeping too. But he left us food and an old plastic bottle full of water."

"You think he's coming back?" She whispered because he did.

"I don't know. He almost made a tunnel out of this place. He set pine branches all along the outside." The boy moved closer to her. "There's something else," he whispered. "Don't get scared or yell or anything, O.K.?"

Amy's stomach knotted as soon as she heard, "Don't get scared," but she said, "I don't yell. What is it?"

"There're people out there—at least I think they're people."

"Where? How close?" She almost breathed the questions.

"I don't know—I just heard 'em talking and moving around. I can't see anything in the dark."

"They're probably looking for Elton and us."

"No . . ." He spoke slowly. "They sound funny. Not like city people."

"What did they say?"

"Grunts mostly, whimpering sounds."

Amy thought that over. "Maybe it was the crazy—James. Maybe he's lost and hurt himself?"

"Wasn't him." The boy was definite. "Besides, there're three or four of them." Somewhere in the darkness a branch snapped. Axel's hand closed over her wrist. "Sh." His breath tickled her ear. Minutes passed, and then she heard the voices and understood Axel's confusion.

"They don't sound like people."

"Animals don't talk."

"That's not talking."

"It's not animals," Axel insisted.

More branches cracked. There was a wicker of wings; birds cried out; there were thudding sounds and hoarse, muffled cries.

"It sounds like they're hunting roosting birds." Axel sat up and Amy did also, as quietly as she could. It seemed a good time to move, while the intruders were occupied. She brushed leaf bits and tiny pebbles from her arms.

The two of them sat in their dark burrow, listening to sounds that suggested a pack of carnivores feeding—animals fighting and snarling and cuffing over their kill. A sudden gust of wind stirred the trees and roused the scents of moss, pine, and clay—and a more familiar scent of long-unwashed human. There was another pervasive odor, which Amy couldn't identify, like sewer gas, but different. What sounded like a child cried out; there was a muffled slap and then wailing.

Axel shifted uneasily. "What do you think they're doing here?" he whispered.

"Like us, maybe?" Amy suggested. "If we got out and the crazy got out, other people must too. Maybe there are a lot of people out here, hiding in the hills."

"But how do they live?"

"How do crazies live in the city?" she countered. "Any way they can. Then they die."

"That's horrible!"

Amy didn't answer; there were a lot of things Axel couldn't understand—and which she could never explain; because he hadn't grown up that way, he never knew. As she would probably never understand his life.

A flash of light interrupted her thoughts and made her jump.

"Heat lightning," Axel whispered. "It's going to rain."

"Rain? How do you know?"

The day had been too warm for June, and nightfall brought no dew. Lightning flickered in the clouds, and now and again a low growl of thunder stilled the crickets and the animal noises.

As the boy explained, Amy felt her fear fade with excitement. It had been her old dream of seeing rain that prompted all this. She was not going to let go by what might be her only chance ever to see this miracle just because she was scared or sunblind. She put her fingers up against her eyes. When the next flash of lightning lit the clouds, she saw it through slits. If she could push the lids up far enough, she reasoned, she could hold them open and protect her eyes from the glare by cupping her hands. And she did.

In her excitement she forgot everything else, including pain and fear; even Axel seemed incidental. There came a flash where she could see the pine branches that screened the ledge. She reached out and pushed a window through them. A drop of water splattered on her hand, and from the distance came the hissing sound of falling rain.

The summer storm was wild and brief, with lightning bolts and thunderclaps and the smell of ozone. The clouds poured rain and hurried on, driven by a high west wind. Amy watched, entranced. It was better, more beautiful than anything she had ever imagined—white and yellow jags of light tearing dark blue clouds, great free claps of thunder noise that made her jump, yet want to shout for joy, silver streaks of water, clouds flickering pink and gray. When the rain drizzled out, the lightning lingered, pulsing here and there, revealing the world for an instant before darkness shut it out again.

Some of the bolts touched down very close to the ledge. Once a tree cracked and flamed, dirt flew, and something screamed in terror as darkness returned. The cry startled Amy from her fantasy. Axel whispered, "It must have hit one of them!" She didn't know what that meant; the light had no violence for her, only beauty. And if all her other dreams about outside failed to come true, at least she had this, the most important one, a glimpse of freedom no authority could ever control.

She was sitting there in the darkness, unconsciously staring in the direction the scream had come from, when the sky lit overhead—and Amy nearly screamed. For in the eerie blue light, cowering not ten feet from her, was the most hideous creature she'd ever seen. Running toward it were two more. And both of those wore something white.

It looked like a hair ball with naked human feet and legs. A well-clawed human hand protruded from that ball to jerk the hair back and reveal a face with mad black-syrup eyes and large crooked teeth in a mouth twisting with hate or fear. The hand and face were caked with blood and dirt. A bird's wing was tangled in the mat of hair and feathers mixed with offal. The creature looked up at the sky and shrieked and ran.

Axel saw only the two pursuers as they passed, and he moved back so quickly that he bumped his head against the concrete overhead. He didn't cry out, for which Amy was grateful, but she heard him whimper as he curled up into fear.

She nearly cried then; he had been so brave ever since that first shaft of sunlight. Now he sounded beaten. She reached out in the dark until she touched him and patted awkward comfort as best she could. And with her other hand she kept one eye open, watching.

The lightning died away and stopped. Minutes passed. From somewhere to the east came a faint screaming noise, and then that stopped. Frogs and crickets went on singing. Mosquitoes whined around her ears. She turned away from the opening in the pines. The air was cooler now, and she felt Axel shivering. She curled up next to him and put her arm around him and felt comforted herself. Somehow things weren't quite so bad if you thought of somebody else's fears. Gradually Axel grew conscious of her enough to grip her hand and hold it tight in both of his. About the time she heard his breathing deepen into sleep, she felt her left arm going numb from lying on it. But she didn't move for fear of waking him. Besides, she told herself, it was warmer this way.

With the soda bubbles in her arm keeping her awake, she thought about those creatures. They were human—she was sure of that—even if they didn't look it. Crazies. But on a scale she'd never imagined. Worse than anything she'd ever seen in the city. Was this what happened to you if you tried to live outside? If there was no one to cut your hair, nothing to cut it with? No clothes to replace those you lost—unless you killed . . . Elton or someone like him? Like her and Axel? And food—where did they find enough to eat? They had no cookers; they had to eat things raw. What else was there besides birds? Insects? She shuddered at that idea.

Maybe what Axel called rabbits—that blood on their faces.
. . . What if Axel couldn't find the way home . . .

Had these people had dreams of outside, too, before'they
left the city? She forced herself to stop thinking then. It was
too frightening. That wouldn't happen to her. . . .

19

The birds woke her in the half light of early dawn. She lay
there listening, wondering how they could still sing after the
slaughter of the night before. But then, she thought, these
were still alive, so why shouldn't they sing so long as they
had the chance?

Axel moved, disturbed by her waking, stiffened, and sat
up. He saw her watching him and managed half a smile.
"Anybody out there?" he whispered.

"Just birds, I think. No crazies." But she whispered too.

He scratched a mosquito welt on his arm and another on
his knee. "Do you think they killed Elton?"

"They had his clothes—or part of them."

He helped himself to the protomush James had left behind, then handed her a wad. "How do you think they killed
him?"

Amy shrugged, not wanting to think, wondering how people like that could get close enough to kill without being
seen. Or smelled. And Elton had had a gun. But maybe he
was like Axel; the way he lived might not have taught him to
be properly afraid of people. "We'll have to watch out for
them and keep away," she said. "Just like with any crazy.
Can you walk?"

"Sure. Can you see again?"

"Pretty well. I made a bandage. See?" Using a rag James had left, she knotted it around her head and pulled the strip down masklike over her face. "I made two rips in it so I can look out," she explained, proud of her ingenuity.

"That looks terrible."

"Who cares?" she said, stung by his criticism. "It keeps my eyelids up and it shades my eyes. We can't sit here and wait to heal. What if those crazies come back?"

Axel looked out at the misty landscape, nervous at the idea of crazies. "What if we leave, and the man—James—comes back here looking for us?"

"Why should he? He doesn't owe us anything." She began stuffing the remains of the protomush into her pockets.

"He might . . . he seems nice. . . ."

"Don't count on it."

"You try to be so tough." Axel sounded a bit exasperated. "You talk as if you didn't like or trust anybody. And you're always pretending things don't matter to you when they matter a lot." Without looking at him, she took a wad of rubbery mush and jammed it halfway into the mouth of the water bottle as an impromptu cork. "When I'm scared, you know and try to make me feel better. I figure to know how scared I am you have to be scared yourself sometimes. But you never act that way. Why is that?"

"What good would it do?" She started to crawl toward the opening in the barricade of branches. "Come on, let's go before the light gets too bright."

"It might make me feel better, knowing I wasn't the only one scared," Axel said, staring at the clay- and grass-stained rumps of her pants. "I know you like me, but sometimes you make me feel like I can't do anything to help you . . . as if you always have to be . . . in charge . . . older—I don't know."

Amy hesitated, one knee off the ground, and stared down at a sow bug moving among the pebbles. Axel was accusing her of something, but she didn't know what, just understanding that he wanted her to be *weak*. She'd always been self-sufficient, as much as she could be. Expecting help from other people didn't pay. But she liked Axel, and she didn't want to make him mad at her.

"How do you want me to act?" she asked.

"Why do you have to *act* at all? Why can't you just be what you are?"

"Because nobody ever likes me that way," she said simply. "They never have. People always want me to act the way *they* would like me to be. Never what I am."

"But I like you the way you are," he insisted.

"Then why do you want me to act scared just because I am?" she said. "I've been scared all my life. I'm used to it. If I acted scared I'd never get anything else done. And it wouldn't change anything. Would it?"

"I guess not," he whispered, confused by the whole conversation but not willing to give up. "I'll tell you what— when I'm really scared I'll just figure you are, too, and then I won't feel like such a baby. O.K.?"

"O.K." She crawled out into the open, looked around cautiously, and stood erect. It felt good to stand after sitting on the ground so long.

"Should we go see where they killed the birds last night?" Axel suggested as he followed her.

"I don't want to—which way is west?"

"See where the sky's pink? The opposite way. The sun rises in the east and sets in the west."

"Right." She remembered then.

"I'll carry the water bottle," Axel volunteered.

The grass and bushes were still wet from the rain. Grasshoppers, sluggish with cold, thudded out of their path. In some spots wet clay clung to their shoes, and wet fabric rubbed their tender feet. After the first half mile of walking, the pain subsided to a bearable degree.

With the morning sun behind them, Amy felt more confident. Her biggest problem was seeing through the frayed slits of her eye shield as she tried to watch for these new and possibly far more dangerous crazy people.

"We're leaving tracks," Axel announced. "If James wants to follow us, he can." The boy pointed back to their blatant path across a muddy stretch.

Amy's first reaction was that she did not particularly want James to follow them, and then she thought, if he could track them, what about the wild crazies? Axel stared at her a moment and then by unspoken mutual agreement, the pair moved up to dryer ground.

They found the air vent quite by chance. It was hidden by a tangle of bushes grown from seeds the wind had brought to rest against its concrete sides—and watered by moisture trapped by the subsurface structure. The children stopped there to have a drink, attracted by the shade, and as they sat and rested they heard wind moaning when there was no breeze. The sound came from the bushes.

At first all they could see was concrete, like the ledge they'd left behind. But when they crawled back into the thicket to investigate, they found a slanted bunker-like structure housing a grille vent. Cool air was whistling out of the vent, air that smelled of machinery and oil, dust and onions.

"It's an air vent for the freight belt!" Axel's whole being

brightened. "All we have to do is find the next one and the next—and follow them home!"

"How do we do that?"

"I don't know." A little of his brightness faded and then resumed. "We'll find a way—I'll crawl up here on the roof. Maybe I can see from there—"

"Careful—the city's old," Amy warned. The concrete was cracked and crumbling.

"This isn't the city," Axel said, pushing sumac fronds aside, looking for a toehold up the grille.

"If you're going I'm going, too." Amy pushed her way to the east end of the structure where the sloping roof almost touched the ground, and there she found a bare spot where no sumac grew. It was the end of a path, like a burrow through the bushes. There were human footprints in the path and strange things on the concrete slab. As she looked at them it reminded her somehow of the things city people put up around their light panels—offerings to a power that might fail.

"What is that stuff?" Axel's whisper made her jump, and she glanced up to see him crawling onto the high end of the vent. "Does some animal sleep here?"

"No. . . ." Amy didn't know what it was—a collection of bones, bottles, and plastic crumples, small animal skulls and fly-covered things she didn't want to examine closely, all arranged in some kind of pattern, but one that made no sense to her. "Maybe a crazy sleeps here," she said. "It might be warm at night—warmer than the ground."

Axel looked down at the path and made a face. "They come here a lot," he agreed. "Maybe every night."

"Let's get out of here."

"O.K." Made nervous by their find, he was about to climb

down, then remembered what he'd climbed up for in the first place. Shading his eyes against the glare, he peered off into the distance in one direction, then another. "There's one back there"—he pointed east—"and that could be a vent, way down there—"

"Let's go." Amy was getting more uneasy by the second. The longer she looked at the stuff on the roof and smelled the dried raw meat, the more she was sure it was dangerous for them to be here. As if eyes were watching them from somewhere in the bushes. "Please?"

"O.K." He came down the sloping roof and paused to give a pile of bones a sideways kick, scattering them into the dirt and leaves. "Disgusting!" Flies buzzed angrily and swarmed after the refuse.

Amy's stomach churned; she wished he hadn't done that. Crazy or not, people didn't like it when you touched their stuff. She turned and headed down the path; it seemed the easiest way out. Then she heard the slap of running feet on clay and saw those feet come into view at the end of the tunnel, blocking her escape. There was a mass of filthy hair—

It had to slow and stoop as it entered the tunnel, but not by much. When it saw her, it growled an angry guttural, bared its teeth, and reached out for her—then saw her mask and hesitated. Its nails were long and curved and black with grime. She heard Axel yell—it was more like a scream— heard him jump to the ground behind her and push into the bushes. She backed into the bushes after him, her eyes never leaving the crazy's. Each time it growled she growled louder with as ugly a sound as she could muster. She had seen a woman do that once, on level nine. The woman had scared off two male crazies who were trying to catch her. This wild crazy seemed to be more mad than scared, and after hesitating at her first growl, it kept coming. She twisted through the thicket, getting scratched and torn but not feeling pain, trying to elude those clawed hands. She pulled a branch back and let it snap across the hairy face. It dodged to save its eyes. Thorns tangled in the hair, and the creature cried out in pain.

"Amy? Was that you?"

"No—Watch out! There may be more outside!"

"I don't see any—"

"We didn't see this one!"

She fell backward out of the thicket, stumbling over roots, rolled onto an elbow and over on her knees. Her tailbone hurt. Something sharp cut through her pants leg and her knee. She felt the cut burn and start to bleed. Axel grabbed her right hand and yanked her up onto her feet. They ran; there was no place to hide.

20

Pulled off-balance by his tugging, she tried to free her hand. He wouldn't let go. "They mustn't catch you! They mustn't catch you!" he kept repeating. "I'd be alone—they mustn't catch you!"

Behind them came the wild thing, and as it ran it made a cry, an *errp! errp!* sound burping up out of its throat, high-pitched and urgent. The noise carried in the stillness, and other voices answered.

"Three more coming!" Amy had looked back.

"Run! They mustn't catch you!"

"*Us!* Catch *us!*"

"No!" He couldn't admit that terror. "Not *me*—I'm not from the city!"

She had no time to understand and did not try. She only knew she could not run far having to compensate for each off-balance step, and if she did not free herself from his protective grip, she would fall and they would both be lost. With effort she forced herself to run fast enough to create a slack in his tugging and then jerked free. He sought her hand again, and she struck out at him.

"Alone," she panted, "run faster alone."

He looked hurt but let her go. Even in panic he led them west, toward home, where safety lay. Through the slits in the rag she wore, Amy saw the ground as a blur where every now and then something sparkled and was gone. Her sides hurt, and her chest, and each yelp of sound behind her struck her stomach like a physical blow.

She could hear their pursuers were getting closer, how close she could not tell, and turning to look back would mean slowing down. The thought occurred to her that the crazies could catch them and weren't. As if they wanted to run them to death—or were playing some vicious game—the sort of game crazy adults played on children in the city when there were no guards around.

Something yelled ahead of them. She looked up, squinted to see, and nearly stopped, despairing. It yelled again. Running toward her was a brown figure that, in her blurred view, had thick wads of hair tangled over one arm and in the other hand carried something shiny.

The crazies behind stopped yelping as if to listen to this new member of the pack. Just then the newcomer slowed and threw what looked like a brown-and-white bag whirling through the air over Amy's head. She heard it thud onto the ground, heard a yelp of surprise and then a growl. The closest footpads stopped; the more distant slowed.

"Amy!" the newcomer called, and Amy's hope returned.

"James!" Excitement and relief nearly choked the words in Axel's throat.

Another brown-and-white thing was thrown at the crazies. "Keep running!" yelled James, and he stopped. As she passed him, Amy saw he held a dead rabbit in one hand and Elton's gun tight in the other. The drawstrings of his bag were tied around his waist. She had gotten perhaps ten yards beyond him when her wind gave out and she staggered to a halt. Axel ran on some distance before he realized he'd lost her and circled back to where she stood.

She turned to look at James. Adjusting her eye rag, which had slipped as she ran, she saw him holding the crazies at bay—two of them, at least. Three more were fighting over the rabbits, pushing and hitting, tugging on the bodies. The two wild men facing James looked at each other, then, as if in an effort to distract him, separated and began to approach from either side.

"I'll kill!"

James aimed directly at the largest one, and both stopped. The large one pulled its hair back to stare at him in what appeared to be a threatening manner, a ritual display of dominance. It was a male. There was a large red welt on its abdomen and sores on its chest and legs.

"Disgusting!" Axel whispered his contempt, but for Amy fear and revulsion mingled with pity for the creature. Those sores must hurt. If she lived out here, alone, for as long as it took hair to grow that long . . . She took a deep breath and wiped sweat from her neck and chin.

"I'll kill!" James warned again. "Go back!"

At that one of the trio fighting over the meat glanced at

James. Its two companions took advantage of its distraction and snatched a rabbit from its grasp. Fur tore and red flashed in the sun. The wild man whirled, picked up a rock, and struck the nearest hairy head a clunk. The victim dropped and lay quite still. The other shrieked and ran, taking all three rabbits; the attacker followed in pursuit.

"Go!" James told the remaining two crazies, but they did not move. The one still covered by its hair scratched vigorously about its waist, then bent down as if to pick up a stone to throw. James aimed and fired. A strip of grass went up in smoke; the wild one froze, hand outstretched. James slowly backed away.

"I don't think they understand words," Axel said when James got close enough to hear.

"Do you? I said run."

"We can't—we're out of breath—"

"Want them to kill you? Run!"

"But you've stopped them," Axel protested.

"For now. There are more. All over."

"I never saw them where I live."

"You don't live here."

"Maybe we better do what James says." Amy was still panting, but the pain had eased in her side and her adrenaline level was up. She felt able to go on.

When he heard her speak his name, her recognition of him as a person, James smiled as if he'd just received a gift. He let the gun falter. The kneeling wild man rose and took a step. James quickly aimed, and the other paused, ready to spring.

"Could you shoot them—just a little—so they can't chase us?" Amy suggested.

James shook his head. "That's cruel. Kinder to kill than wound. Infection makes slow dying here."

"They'd kill us," said Axel. "Look at them!"

"Poor animals," said James, and something in his tone made Amy like him. He sounded the way she felt when she wondered if she could live out here alone. And it occurred to her, in that glimpse of growing up, that it must have been hard to live the way James did, friendless, exposed to stares and contempt and rats. And he had been born above and sent down, and that was worse. No wonder he seemed crazy. Axel was afraid he would grow up to live like that. For James it had come true.

"Haah-ah!"

The piercing scream was intended to startle, to frighten— and it did—and with that cry both wild men came for them in a rush. Perhaps, as wild things will, they sensed James's empathy, his reluctance to kill, and mistook that empathy for weakness.

Distracted by her own thoughts, Amy was so frightened by the scream that her heart skipped a beat, and for that instant time seemed to stop. She saw the three of them—James and the two wild men—in slow ballet. James hesitating, aiming first at one, then the other, not wanting to kill. She was aware of hairy legs, with bald knees flashing out of hair skirts, filthy hands with talon fingers, lips drawn back ape-like to bare teeth as the shrieks crescendoed.

The hands were reaching out to tear and grab. She saw the blue laser flash repeatedly. One body leaped aside, writhing, hands clutching at its middle as if to tear out pain. It fell to the ground convulsing, and went still. It was the lucky one. The other tried to dodge the beams, and the lethal light pierced its hair. The hair, filthy with years of body oil and animal fat, ignited and blazed up. The creature twisted, ran, and fell. The final screams were human. James fired again, three times, as if to correct a terrible mistake, and then, very like his victims, cried out and sank down on his knees, convulsed by sobs. The gun fell from his hand and clanked against a stone.

Amy had never seen a man cry before, never seen anyone cry like this, and if she had not been so deep in shock it would have frightened her. James cried as if his heart would break, as if everything he'd ever suffered never had been given voice. Beside her Axel turned away to be sick on the grass. She stood dumb, looking from one to the other, and then decided James needed help more. There wasn't much that she could do except put her hand on his shoulder. He was shaking, and his skin felt cold through his shirt, although he was drenched with sweat.

When he became aware of her, he tried to talk. The words were interrupted by his sob reflex, and when she finally understood them, they had no meaning for her then. "They brought me down to their level," he sobbed. "They brought me down. They brought me down."

She knew he didn't refer to the dead men, but then to whom?

The wind blew and brought the smoke and scent of what had burned swirling their way. Amy sniffed and wiped her nose and looked around to find Axel. He was sitting on the ground, looking pale and exhausted, his eyes great circles in his little face. Perhaps a quarter of a mile away three wild men stood in a row on a knoll, watching.

"We have to go, James," she decided. "We can't stay here. You have to get up now." She patted the sweat-soaked shoulder of his shirt. "We're going home to Axel's place. You have to help us get there. You can't sit here and cry. We've come too far for that."

He raised his head and looked up at her. Weeping had washed some of the madness from his soul, mind and muscles had relaxed, and his brief smile when it came was beautiful. As he looked at her, his eyes filled again. He swallowed audibly, and his Adam's apple jerked. He nodded in affirmation and pushed himself to his feet.

She picked up the gun and held it out to him. He shook his head. "Yes," she said. "We'll need it." He shook his head again. Amy hesitated, then, making sure it was turned off, stuck the gun in her pocket. "Come on," she said and took his hand. "Let's go." He nodded again and then reached down and helped Axel to his feet.

"Come on," James said. "We're going home."

21

Amy trudged along half asleep, aware of the other two, but barely. The smell of them, the sound of their footsteps, the whisper of moving fabric came through her consciousness, but that was all. Her body moved on automatic pilot.

They passed more ventilator shafts, giving these thicketed places wide berth, fearing what might be hiding there. They walked in the open, often looking back. They were being followed at a distance.

No birds sang, but now and then one would racket up in panic from a nest in the grass and frighten the three walkers. The breeze died. Flies and bees zoomed by, exuberant in the warm sunshine.

Sometimes Amy would see what resembled a fuzzy hornet's nest bobbing along a hillside, and as she watched, it would stop or duck out of sight behind a tree. When that happened she got a sick feeling in her stomach. Suppose the crazies attacked and she had to kill them? She wasn't sure she could. She considered giving Axel the gun—and some instinct warned her not to. He hadn't shut out for a long time now, but just in case . . .

A sound made her glance at James and squint to see him fumbling in the bag he carried. He withdrew the floppy white cloth hat she recognized as Elton's, shook it out, and put it on Axel's head. It nearly covered the boy's eyes. Axel was startled and yanked it off. The underside of the limp brim was stiff with a red-brown stain.

"What is that?" The boy held the thing gingerly between two fingers, at arm's length.

"A hat." James spoke for the first time in hours. "Wear it, for your eyes."

"No! It's bloody!"

"It's dry."

"It's disgusting!" Axel let the hat fall. "They bashed his head in!"

"Yes." James retrieved the hat, put it on, reached into the bag again, and held out Elton's sunglasses to Amy. She didn't want to hurt his feelings, but neither did she want to wear those glasses.

"You wear them," she said. "Your eyes are sore, too, and you have to see to take care of us. My rag's fine—it holds my eyes open. Those won't."

"These are better," he said. "Clean. No blood."

"You wear them, please?"

He hesitated, his eyes searching her face as if trying to judge her sincerity. Then he nodded and put on the glasses. They walked on for a mile or more. Then Amy stumbled and fell over a vine, and it took the other two to pull her up. The effort left them so exhausted that they stopped to rest there and ate the mush Amy had in her pockets.

She was so tired she could hardly chew. Only fear of what

might happen if she fell asleep kept her awake. And thirst. The water bottle was gone, left behind in their flight from the thicket. She sat looking at the empty land and wondered where the crazies were. That reminded her; she pulled the gun out of her pocket and lay it where it could be quickly grabbed if any of them tried to rush the hill.

James's glasses glinted in the sun as he looked around and stared at the weapon. With a sigh he reached out and picked it up and put it in his pocket. "Children shouldn't have to kill," he said, and pushed himself up on his feet.

The afternoon was hard. Sun and fatigue made progress very slow. All three staggered as they walked. Once Axel sank down on his knees, and Amy thought he'd fallen, only to have him get up and hand her an olive-green and speckled pebble.

"Eat it," he said, and picked up two more from a pile of twigs. She was sure then that he had gone from weird to crazy.

"You can't eat rocks," she said.

"It's an egg." He was tired and impatient. "Don't be stupid. Birds lay eggs, like chickens." She stared at him, ignorant. "Like this." He carefully tapped one pebble against the other, and one broke. Inside, a yellow ball floated in thick water—and he drank it. He took her pebble back and cracked it. "Open your mouth," he ordered, and when she did, he poured the water in. It had a funny, stringy taste. She watched to see how James liked his. He held it in his mouth awhile and then swallowed with a gulp.

"Raw," he said. "I never had eggs raw."

"You know what they are?" Axel was surprised.

James nodded. "Long time ago. Before they sent me down." The man smiled, as if pleased by the memory. "More eggs?" he asked.

"I guess so." Axel looked around. "If we can find them. I never thought of it—I should have. We can look as we walk."

"We better," James said. "No more mush."

"None in your bag?"

He shook his head.

They had to rest every ten minutes or so after that. Each stop got longer as the hills grew steeper. Axel foraged as he went and found a variety of eggs, almost all tiny. Amy tried but couldn't see well enough to find anything but a few strawberries—and those only because the bright red color caught her eye. James shot at six birds and missed them all, inexperienced at small swift targets.

"How did you shoot the rabbits?" Axel asked wonderingly.

"They were eating. Sitting still."

At last they came to an upgrade steeper than any they'd climbed before. By the time they reached the top, Amy knew she couldn't go any farther. She sank down on a patch of wild oats. One frond poked her in the ear. It tickled but she was too tired to move or even scratch. She just sat there, staring like a lumpen at the ventilator housing on the downside of the hill. Axel sat down nearby but James stood.

"If I sit down, I won't get up again," he said.

She wondered if he meant he was going to die there, and she squinted up at him. He was beginning to look the way she remembered—filthy dirty and unshaven, his eyes haggard. He was breathing harder than she was.

"Are you O.K.?" she asked, not sure what she meant by that.

"No," he said between breaths. "But we—need fire. To keep—long-haired ones away in the dark. I'll get trees."

It was almost sunset by the time they'd gathered all the dry brush they could find, carried it to the center of the hilltop and stacked it in low piles around them. In the fading light they saw two wild men in the distance running after something and calling. James thought they were hunting rabbits or birds to eat.

"At least they aren't chasing us," said Axel. "Can we light the fire?"

He had arranged a small pile of brushwood on a bare spot of clay, assuring the two city dwellers that he had often done this before. It was called camping. When James aimed the laser and set the twigs on fire, the flames licked up cheerfully. But after a few minutes' burning, more smoke than flame appeared, the smoke redolent with the green pine boughs in the fire's heart. The three moved back out of the cloud and watched it rise in a column on the still evening air.

"It'll quit smoking," Axel said, cheered by the light. "Wait till it dries a little." He divided up the birds' eggs he'd found, five for each, and Amy parceled out seven berries among them, and that was their supper. It was just enough to aggravate their hunger pains, but it quenched some of their thirst.

They sat, each one facing a different way, backs to the smoking fire, listening to their stomachs growl, resting, forcing themselves to stay awake and watch.

"Why would the crazies kill Elton?" Axel broke a long silence. "He wasn't hunting them."

"Maybe they thought he was."

"Maybe—they remember?" James said unexpectedly. "I was sent down. Others are put out. Exiled, like you. Taken to the city's edge and driven off by guards in white. To make sure no one came back to the domes. Some did. Starving. Hurled themselves against the glass. Begging to be let in again. I saw them. I was a child. . . ." His voice trailed off.

"Why didn't the authorities just kill them and get it over with?" asked Amy.

"To teach the ones inside. To frighten—to make them glad to go down into darkness."

"Are there many outside?"

"No. Or we would see more."

Amy didn't understand that, but it didn't matter. "Elton followed us to make sure we got away?" she asked.

"No," James said. "To make sure you didn't come back."

"Oh." She thought about that for a while, then, "James? How old were you when they sent you down to our level?"

"Seven."

"How old are you now?"

His face clouded. "I don't know . . . I did . . . I lost count . . . sleeping . . . watching. The lights were always on . . ."

She saw that she was confusing him, making him think back into the dark years. "It doesn't matter," she said quickly. "I just wondered. Valory—my mother—she's twenty-seven."

He didn't say anything for a while, and his gaunt face retained its troubled look. Then he asked, "When Janet died—how old were you?"

"Eight."

"How long ago?"

"Three years."

"That's all?"

It seemed a very long time to her, but she said, "Yes. I'm eleven now."

"I was twenty-six the last time I saw Janet."

"You're twenty-nine then." He looked very old to her, much older than her mother.

"Twenty-nine," he said wonderingly. "I lived to be *old*.

The guard told me, 'You're getting old.' I didn't believe her."

"That's not *old*." Axel turned and stared at him. "There're people where I live three times that old."

"Why?" said James

Axel frowned. "They just are—what do you mean why?"

"How can they?"

Axel didn't know how to reply, and then he grinned. "You'll see," he promised. "It's a very nice place. You'll live to be a hundred."

"Will I want to?" James asked in all seriousness.

"Everybody does," the boy assured him.

James thought that over. "But they belong there." He spoke slowly, as if trying to articulate something more difficult than usual for him. "They were *born* there. I wasn't. If I go there—maybe they won't want a crazy around? No one does. Not even other crazies. They might not like it if I live that long . . . drive me away. . . ."

"They won't!" Axel denied it vehemently. "You're not a crazy—not really. Not any more than I am. The city makes people be—ugly, be—" He couldn't think clearly what he felt to be true. "It makes you things you wouldn't be if you weren't there," he concluded lamely, and then brightened at another thought. "You'll be a hero—both of you—when they hear all you've done for me. You saved my life."

Amy listened to this exchange and thought her own thoughts. She couldn't imagine Axel's world any more than she could imagine anyone feeling gratitude for any act of hers. Her experience with people had taught her to expect either hostility or indifference. Janet had been the only exception, the only person who cared, and Amy wondered what Janet would think if she could see where her dreams of "outside" had led. She stared down at a clotted brier scratch on her left foot. Suppose James's fears were right, that Axel's people would not want them. Her eyes closed to shut out the despair induced by exhaustion, and she dozed off.

A sound woke her and she jumped, heart pounding. It was dark. She clutched at the rag around her eyes and pulled it up to see the blurry light of a dying fire. She reached out, felt the brush pile next to her, tore loose a dry branch and laid it on the flickering light. Smoke billowed out into her face. Her eyes teared and she began to cough. On the other side of the fire James gave a mighty snort of a snore and jumped up as he came awake, conditioned by years of being kicked by passersby. For an instant he stared wild-eyed at Amy, then remembered where he was and felt his pocket for the gun.

"Yes?" he whispered and nodded toward the night around them.

"I don't know—a sound—"

Something whizzed past her and struck the fire. Sparks flew up. A pebble hit Axel's back with a soft thud, and he whimpered in his sleep and curled into fetal position. James pressed the trigger. Blue beams drew lines in the darkness. In reply the top half of a bottle hit and shattered in the fire. James aimed in the direction it had come from. "Get down!" he ordered Amy. A stone just missed his head.

Dead leaves and pine needles in the grass downhill caught fire; tiny flames flickered. Most were stillborn, but a few lasted long enough to ignite larger things. A pine cone caught and blazed and set alight the pine branch it clung to. A fringe of fire began to creep through the grass. A guttural outcry was the first sound from their attackers. Amy saw a shadow run silhouetted against the smoky light.

"Set more grass on fire, James!" she called out to him. "Make 'em run to get away from it!"

He followed her suggestion, as ignorant as she, as unthinking, until runnels of flame nearly encircled the hilltop.

Downhill a wax-thorn torched. A warm wind breathed to life, and the flames danced beneath the smoke. Amy was sorry the light hurt her eyes; the flames were full of pretty colors—greens and blues and oranges.

"What is he doing?" Axel startled her with a frightened whisper.

"They were throwing rocks! Trying to hit us!" Amy explained. "James is chasing them with fire!"

"He'll burn us all!" Axel stood up, agitated. A rock flew over them, and Amy yanked him down.

"It's all right," she said. "There's no grass right here—"

"You don't understand!" Axel was half in tears. "You've never seen a grass fire! It can move so fast—you can't outrun the flames! You can't breathe smoke—"

"We don't have to—just the crazies have to."

The boy looked at her and shook his head. "Stupid!

Amy didn't understand why he couldn't appreciate the cleverness of their defense. It got rid of the wild men without having to kill them, and it offered protection.

The fire gained a life of its own. In ten minutes their hilltop was ringed by flames, some moving downhill, some creeping sideways. The rock-throwing had stopped. Birds squawked or sang bewilderedly in the darkness. Frightened field mice squeaked. A rabbit ran in panic. Grass wilted and smoked, while last year's dry underlayer caught and flamed. Hot air rose and roiled up through the smoke to become a wind. The breeze was from the south.

Amy thought the ground was shaking, but she couldn't be sure. Lately her body had done a lot of shaking on its own. She pressed her hand flat against the clay and felt vibrations. It reminded her of the way the walls shook in the city at night. Was the outside old, too?

"Look!" Axel pointed toward the ventilator thicket. It was

burning and a path of flame stretched from there halfway up the hill. "Bins are moving in the freight tunnels down below! Pushing air out of the shafts! Feel the ground shaking? That's—"

The fire wind gusted. A cloud of smoke and soot enveloped them, and Axel's excitement ended in a coughing spasm. Amy choked and turned away, eyes and lungs burning. What had been air was suddenly all smoke. She jumped up in panic, into the thick of the cloud, and ran, eyes tearing, whimpering as her bare feet and ankles touched hot spots of charred sod.

She ran where there was no flame—for flame was the only thing she could see. She fell and rolled and crawled, a terror-stricken animal desperate for oxygen. Nothing and no one else existed for her now. She reached a strip of burning grass, stood up and tried to jump the flames. Her left foot caught under something as she landed, and pitched her, face down. She rose again, spitting dirt, swallowed the sourness welling in her throat, and took two more steps before her left knee buckled. When she hit the ground this time, nothing hurt. Her head struck against a rock.

22

It was almost daylight, a misty dawn gray with smoke and fog. She sat up, wet, stiff, and cold. Her head throbbed, and her chest hurt with each breath. When she touched her forehead, her fingers met a sticky lump. The dirt and ashes on her hand made the open gash burn. "That wasn't smart," she told herself, and the sound of her own voice scared her. What if there were still crazies around?

From what she could see, she was alone, sitting on a bare stretch of clay at the bottom of the hill. All around her stretched blackened grass. A few pines had survived the fire and stood isolate, dark patches in the mist. Unsure if all the fuzziness was fog or her eyesight, she blinked again and again. Her vision did not clear, and she gave up. It was time to find Axel and James.

At first, not trusting herself to stand, she tried to crawl back up the hill, but her left knee hurt so much that she had to stop. After three tries she managed to stand more or less erect. While waiting for the dizziness to subside, she heard a strange noise and remembered hearing it before. The same sound had wakened her—a high-pitched whine combined with dry snapping noises, like branches breaking.

All she could see from here were hills and fog. Nothing moved. Maybe it was coming from the freight tunnel, she thought, and set off up the hill, pausing every few steps because her head throbbed so.

Halfway up, she saw a wild crazy sprawled on the ground, face down. She could not be sure that it was dead, but it did not move. After waiting a few minutes, she went on. The whining sound grew louder.

James and Axel lay almost where she'd left them, near the ashes of their original fire. Most of the brush they'd gathered lay unburned. The fire had never reached it. James was in the same position in which he used to sleep in the passageway outside her door on level nine, curled up to protect himself from kicks. The only difference was that his right hand was gripping Axel's ankle, as if to keep the boy from running.

She couldn't see their faces clearly until she squatted beside them and braced herself with her hands to keep from pitching forward. She held her hand in front of Axel's mouth and felt his shallow breath warm on her fingers. It was too far to reach across him to James, so she stared at the man's chest until she saw it rise and fall. Satisfied they were still alive, she pushed herself erect again and turned in the direction the noise seemed to be coming from.

A light rain began. The cold drops plunked on her head. Like a benumbed animal, she raised her face to try to drink. Then something appeared out of the fog, several hundred yards away. Five minutes passed before she saw it was a huge green vehicle mounted on four black doughnut-shaped wheels that carried the box-like cab high above the brush. It rolled along very slowly, as if unsure of itself.

"Axel?" she whispered. "Axel? Wake up! Someone's coming!" When Axel did not answer, she looked down at him and then gently nudged his shoulder with her bare foot. "Axel?" She nudged a little harder. "Axel, wake up. Please!" But Axel did not answer. "James?" She tried to waken him, but he too would not rouse. She crouched behind the brush pile to watch.

Bright yellow lights came on from the front of the vehicle and focused on the blackened housing of the ventilator shaft. The whining noise diminished as the unit slowed and stopped. Almost immediately a door slid open in the cab and three people, one after another, emerged to climb down a four-step ladder to the ground.

They were all dressed in different colors. Amy couldn't identify their job class or even be sure they were wearing uniforms. A fourth person, still in the cab, dropped something bright yellow down to each of them. She'd never seen rain capes before and didn't know what they were, but she liked the way they looked. The trio walked over to the ventilator and circled around it.

"The fire started here," one called, "from the outside."

"Lightning?"

"No sign of that."

There was something familiar in the tone, in the slow cadence of their speech. Axel talked like that. It occurred to her that these might be his people, or at least outside people. That car was much too big to go inside the city, even in the domes.

"Axel?" She turned to crawl back to where he lay. "Axel! You've got to wake up! I think it's *them*—your people! You've got to look!" She shook him as hard as she could, which wasn't much, but he did not or could not respond.

She glanced from his still face to the glow of yellow in the fog below. If he didn't get help soon, he was going to die, she thought, he and James—and herself, too. But if she called out to the strangers and they were from the city . . . then it was all over. Yet if they were Axel's people and she let them go away— She took as deep a breath as she could, stood up, and, weaving like a drunk, set off down the slope.

What did one say to total strangers in a case like this? she wondered, suddenly as shy as she was scared. Hello, are you from the city? Hello, do you know anyone who lost a boy? And if they were his people, what would they think of her?

"Look!" The man in the cab called and pointed. "Up there! On the hill!"

The three yellow capes stopped moving, and Amy felt her stomach cramp with nerves. She felt rather than knew definitely that they were staring at her. For a moment she hesitated, then staggered on. It was too late now to change her mind.

"It's a child!"

"How did it get out here?"

"It can hardly go any more. Look at the way it's walking."

"It's hurt!"

She saw them start to run toward her, and she stopped,

frightened as much by their remarks as by their sudden rush. Did she look as bad as they implied? Before she had time to worry about it, they loomed up in front of her. One dropped to his knees and reached out to take her hands. She pulled back at his touch.

"Don't be afraid," he said. "We won't hurt you."

"Who are you? How did you get here?" asked another.

She looked up at the blur that was their faces. "My name is Amy," she said, slowly and distinctly so she wouldn't have to waste energy repeating things. "We walked—from the city. Axel and James and me."

None of them responded, and she couldn't see their expressions to guess what their reactions were. The knots in her stomach tightened.

"You walked from the city? You and other children?" one of them asked. "You crossed the wastelands?"

"Axel and me. And James—but we met him outside."

"James is a man—an adult?" the same man asked.

"We can get the details later," the kneeling man said briskly. "Let's find her friends and see what kind of shape they're in."

"They're sleeping," Amy said. "I can't make them wake up."

There was another little silence, and then the man beside her rose and brushed off his knees. "Maybe we can," he said. "Why don't you show us where they are?"

"You're not from the city, are you?" She wanted to be sure.

"No. We live in—well, you wouldn't recognize the name, but over there some fifteen miles." He pointed west.

"Oh. O.K." As she turned to lead them up the slope again, she stumbled and two of the men caught her by the arms. "It's O.K. I can walk," she said.

"I know," the man who'd knelt replied, "but we can help a little."

She automatically looked up to see if he was mocking her, but she couldn't see well enough to tell.

"You've got yourself a bad burn, Amy," he observed. "Is that from the sun—or this fire?"

"The sun," she said. "Axel said it burned."

"I found them." The third man had walked on ahead of Amy and her escorts and now called, "You'd better wave to Charley to bring the tractor up. This man's going to need help."

"Who's that down there?" The second man pointed.

"He's naked—look at that hair. . . ."

"That's one of the wild crazies," Amy told them. "I think he's dead."

"Wild crazy?"

"They've been chasing us," she explained. "That's why we started the fire—to make them go away again."

"Where did they come from?" the man beside her asked. "The city too?"

"James says they did. A long time ago. The authorities sent them out so they'd die, but they didn't. Not all of them."

"Do you know what she's talking about, Dave?"

Amy made a mental note—the man who had knelt in front of her was named Dave, and of the three he seemed the most friendly, but he also seemed not to want to say too much in front of her. Like now, when he told the other man, "No, but we can discuss that later. Let's get everybody in the truck and get out of here."

"Right!"

"Come over here and look at this," the lead man called. "He looks like an animal—"

"Is he definitely dead?" Dave called back.

"Yeah."

"Then let's check out those two first."

"Yeah, O.K., but—" Reluctantly the third man rejoined them.

Dave turned and beckoned to the car below. The big vehicle made a whining noise and slowly began to move up the slope at an oblique angle. Amy watched as the man dropped to one knee beside Axel, who lay on his stomach, his head pillowed on his arm.

"He's still breathing," he announced after a bit. "Let me move him first so we have room to work on the man." He loosened James's grip on the boy's ankle, then reached under Axel with both hands, lifted, and turned him over. "We'll get him . . ."

For a second Amy thought someone had hit the man because he jerked violently and then dropped to both knees and made a funny sound, but she hadn't seen anybody else move.

"What is it, Dave?" his friend asked. "You hurt?"

"I think it's Michael! Under all that crud—It's Michael! It's Michael!" The other two men leaned over to look at Axel's face. "He's so thin. . . ."

"It sure looks like him," one man agreed.

"It's Michael," Dave repeated, and as he lifted Axel to cradle him close, the boy moved.

"Dad?" Amy heard Axel say. "How did you get here?" and then Dave sounded like he had started to laugh but the sound ended more like he was going to cry. Axel reached up and touched the man's face. "I'm so glad to see you!" he said. "I was afraid I'd never see you again. I tried and tried to get out, and then Amy—" He went still and then twisted in his father's arms. "Amy! She ran into the fire! The smoke was so thick, and she ran, and I went after her but I couldn't find her. I looked and looked, and then James brought me back and wouldn't let me hunt any more. And he got burned and I think she's dead—" His voice broke.

"No, Michael—Michael? Listen—"

"She didn't answer, Dad. She saved my life, and now she's dead—"

"She's here, Michael. Right over there."

"She came to get us, son," one of the other men said. "She's alive. Come over here, Amy, so he can see you." And with an exuberant swoop, the man lifted Amy off her feet and set her down beside the pair. The shock of being lifted, along with the abrupt up-and-down movement, was the last thing Amy needed at the moment. She saw Axel reach out a hand toward her and knew he was talking, but she couldn't hear the words for the buzzing in her head. The world went gray; she felt a big arm go around her waist, and then nothing.

23

"What's your name?" a voice asked over and over. She wouldn't tell them. They asked that in Rehabilitation—"What's your name? What's your name?"—to see if you remembered. Her head hurt, slow waves of pain.

"That's Amy," Axel said. He was trying to help her, to make them quit hurting her. He had come back for her . . . she couldn't remember when. Water was running down her face. Tears. Her eyes were burning with them.

"We want *her* to tell us her name, Michael—to wake her up. It's been three days now," a woman said.

"She's tired. She's just sleeping!" It *was* Axel's voice; Amy was sure of that. Why did they call him that other name? "Amy—wake up! Amy?" He was squeezing her hand. She tried to squeeze back, but it took so much effort that she gave up and fell asleep again. Voices murmured in her dreams, endless dreams, dark and frightening, pointless.

Her nose itched, and she scratched it. It itched again. "Bug," she heard herself whisper, and someone said, "No. Me." She opened her eyes. The light was dim. James was sitting close by her bunk, his elbows on the mattress. She stared at him, not understanding how he'd gotten here.

"Don't be afraid," he said. "We're safe. There are no bugs. Nothing bad. Not any more."

He was neat and clean and wearing a blue shirt. There were white bandages on both arms. They were clean too. His eyes were clear and full of peace.

"No!" He leaned forward and touched her cheek. He smelled of soap. "Don't go back to sleep. Not yet. For me?"

It seemed important to him. "Am I awake?" she tried to ask. Her voice sounded strange, and she licked her lips. James reached over and got a glass of water from somewhere and put the straw in her mouth. Her lips felt like paper.

"Drink. Very slowly."

The water woke her up, cool and clear. She was in a strange room. There were pictures on the wall. Flowering plants grew by a window. The room was painted white, and she was covered with a yellow cloth. Everything was clean— as clean as James. As clean as her own arms, which lay stretched out on the cloth.

"What's that tube in my arm?" She had just noticed it. The thing was taped against the inside of her left wrist, and led to a shiny bottle of water hanging from a rack overhead.

"Food," said James. "You could not eat. They had to give your body food."

She considered that. "It looks like water."

"Yes," James agreed. "Doesn't taste like it."

"Is it good?"

"Sweet."

"Oh," she said.

"Do you know my name?"

"James." Had he forgotten his own name?

"Do you know your name?"

She stared at him; poor man. "Amy. My name is Amy."

"Yes!" He smiled and patted her hand.

"Where's Axel?"

"In bed. Asleep. It's late at night."

"Is he O.K.?"

"A few burns. Weak. Like us. But we're *alive*."

That fact seemed to surprise him, she thought. Maybe if she thought about it more she would understand why. She turned her head and looked around the room. It was good to be able to see again.

"Are you still awake?"

"Yes."

"I will tell you where we are. And how. So you know."

"O.K." It would be nice to listen to a story. Her mind was drifting in and out of awareness.

"One of the boy's people saw the fire. Way off in the dark. The hill burning. Then smoke came into the freight yards— from the tunnels. They thought the tunnels were burning. They came to see. And found us."

He paused in his story to give her more water. "You were hurt worst. Your head—and smoke breathing. They—"

"Four men, with a big green car . . ." Amy was remembering now.

"Yes. They have a big car. High wheels to carry them through mud and brush. We were put inside . . . I don't remember that—they told me so when I woke up. Here."

"The hairy crazies—did they chase the car too?"

James shook his head. "No . . . they were gone. All but one. Dead. They'd never seen a man like that before. Just heard of them. But didn't want to believe . . ." He paused in thought. "They went back—to bury him, they said. And take pictures. But he was gone. We had to tell them over and over, the boy and I. How they look. How they make sounds . . . about their hair. . . . They'll ask you, too. . . ."

"Are we with Axel's people?"

"Yes."

"Is it like he said?"

"I don't remember. It's good. You'll like it."

"Do they *mind* our being here? You and me? We could sneak away—"

"No!" For him the tone was almost emphatic. "They want us. They said so—especially you. The boy told them how you came to get him and helped him come home. They cried. They come in here and watch you sleep, and they cry." He frowned. "I don't know why they cry so much. Sometimes when I talk they cry. Or get angry. Not at me. I don't understand them sometimes. . . . They cannot change what is . . . the city . . . the authorities. Not without being cruel. And they seem kind."

Amy couldn't follow all that. She bit her upper lip in muddled thought. "Do they have food and water enough for us too? And a place to sleep?"

James's smile was her answer. It covered his whole face and made him look as young as he was. "So much food! And a lake of water. Blue. Fountains—you will see, Amy. You never saw beautiful before, but you will see it. Beautiful land. Beautiful people. Big and strong and healthy."

"Will Axel be ashamed of us?" she asked. "We're not

beautiful—and we—I—don't know so many things. He called me stupid."

"No." He took both her hands and held them tight. "Don't be afraid now. We've lived through the worst time of our lives. Anything will be better. We will be allowed to *read* . . . see?" He reached over behind her bed and held up a book and then another and another. "For you. To keep. Gifts from the people here. And for me too." He smiled. "We can read anything."

"They'd let us do that? Learn anything?" She looked at the books. They were clean and didn't smell.

"Yes. And there are more gifts. Flowers there." He pointed. "And clothing—in the closet. And toys. All for you."

"What's a toy?"

He frowned, not able to explain, and then stood up slowly, favoring one leg.

"Are you hurt?"

"Burned. Not bad. Just my feet and legs." He crossed the room to a door and slid it open. She saw he was wearing blue shorts and his legs were mottled black-and-red scars from the knees on down. The lighting was too dim for her to see more than a blur of colors in the closet. James pushed clothes aside, then turned to her. "The boy's mother said . . ." He paused to remember the words. "It was the custom to close your eyes . . . and hold out your hands . . . and get a surprise. So do that."

"Do what?"

"Close your eyes. Then I tell you when to open them."

She stared at him. "What are you going to do?"

"A surprise. A nice one."

"O.K." She closed her eyes and listened to him shut the closet door and come back to the bed, then felt something furry touch her hand. She jerked away, thinking of rats; her eyes flew open. There on the bed, regarding her with large black-and-white eyes, sat a round brown-and-beige animal with furry ears, a shiny nose, and a red cloth tongue.

"What is it?"

"A teddy bear. It's a toy."

She looked at it more closely and ran a finger over the furry ears and head. It felt good.

"What do I do with it?"

"She said it was to sleep with. When you felt lonely. You hold it, and it helps you to go to sleep. She said it keeps bad dreams away."

"Does it work?"

"Yes," said James. "I told her I had bad dreams and she gave me one. And it works. Mine's blue."

Amy stared at the bear. It stared back, unblinking.

"The funny thing is," James continued, "when I told her this morning that the teddy bear worked, she got tears in her eyes. She pretended she didn't. But I saw them."

Amy didn't answer. She had pulled the bear up so that she could pillow her cheek against its sturdy head. It felt soft and warm. She closed her eyes to think about all the things James had told her. She heard him ease back into his chair.

"James?"

"Yes?"

"Where will we live? Here?"

"No. This is a medix place." He gestured toward the window. "Out there. With Michael's people. That's his name now. Michael. They have a big house, and we'll have our own rooms. With beds. I saw it today." He smiled again at the memory.

"What will we do here?"

"Live. Live to be a hundred. The boy was right. They do."

Amy was thinking again. "If it's late at night, why aren't you in bed?"

He looked down at the floor, suddenly bashful. "I came in to see you. The medic was tired. I said I'd sit with you. Call them if you woke . . . oh?" He remembered his promise and reached for the bell.

"Do you have to?"

"Yes—no."

"It's O.K.?"

"Yes. Besides, let her sleep. She can see you in thé morning." He stretched his legs slowly. "We'll talk—you and I."

"James?"

"Yes?"

"I'm very hungry."

"Yes?" He pushed himself up out of the chair again and winced. "You won't fall asleep?"

"Where are you going?"

"To get food."

"I'll stay awake." Her stomach rumbled at the thought of something to eat. The more she thought about it, the wider awake she became. She watched James go out the door, watched the door slide shut behind him, and suddenly felt fear. She was all alone. In a very strange place. Suppose a stranger came in? What would she say to them? What if James didn't come back? She hugged the bear tight against her. Then the door slid open and she felt foolish.

"Food," James whispered. He carried a tray, and on it were a pile of things and two glasses of liquid. "Sandwiches and ginger ale.

"Eat slowly," he cautioned, and she did. It tasted too good to swallow fast. But the odd thing was, for all she thought she was starved, she couldn't eat much, and she drank only half her ginger ale before she wanted to go to sleep again. She didn't tell James for fear he'd want to talk some more. She just closed her eyes.

When she woke again, the tray was gone. James was snoring in his chair, her teddy bear sitting on his lap, watching her. She lay there listening to birds sing and watching dawn turn the window blue. The lawn outside came green with sunlight. The door slid open softly, and she turned her head to see Axel standing there.

When he saw her looking at him, he began to grin. "Are you awake?" he whispered.

"Yes."

"Are you going to live?"

"Yes! What sort of question is that?"

Without another word, he turned and ran out, leaving the door open. A few seconds later, she saw him running past the window, and as he ran he shouted, "Mom! Dad! Wake up! Everybody! Amy's going to live!"

It was over; the whole long daydream about going outside was ended. She was here. And it was nothing like she'd imagined it to be. The world in Janet's battered book was gone as surely as those pages. But like the woman and her book, this world was real and offered hope, and she would make it hers. It might take a while, Amy thought, and it might be hard, but she had come up from level nine, and after that, anything was easy.

Orson Scott Card

ENDER'S GAME

Winner of the Hugo Award
Winner of the Nebula Award
An American Library Association
"100 Best Books for Teens"

Ender Wiggin has hardly had a childhood when representatives of the world government recruit him for military training at a facility called Battle School. A genius, Ender is considered a master strategist. His skills will be necessary if the Earth can repel another attack by alien Buggers. In simulated war games Ender excels. But how will he do in real battle conditions? After all, Battle School *is* just a game, right?

"Superb." — *Booklist*

ENDER'S SHADOW

2000 Alex Award Winner
An American Library Association
"Top 10 Best Book"

Life on the streets is tough. But if Bean has learned anything it's how to survive. Not with his fists. Bean is way too small to fight. But with his brain. Like his colleague and rival Ender Wiggin, Bean has been chosen to enroll in Battle School. And like Ender, Bean will be called upon to perform an extraordinary service. A parallel novel to the extraordinary *Ender's Game*.

"An exceptional work." — *School Library Journal*

H. M. Hoover

ORVIS

An American Booksellers
"Pick of the Lists"

Parents Choice Children's Media
Award for Literature

When Toby stumbles upon an abandoned robot named Orvis, she knows exactly how he feels. No one wants her either. With Orvis and her only friend Thaddeus—another lonely castoff—Toby sets off across the vast Empty in search of sanctuary.

"A first-rate adventure."—*Parents Choice*

ANOTHER HEAVEN, ANOTHER EARTH

An American Library Association
"101 Best of the Best Books in the Past 25 Years"

"Superb!"—*The Times Educational Supplement*

Only a handful of residents remain on Xilan from the original crew that colonized the planet centuries before. Including Gareth. When a rescue mission arrives from Earth, however, Gareth must make a difficult decision: accept their help and abandon the only past she has ever known . . . or cling to the past and risk extinction.

"A real blockbuster of a novel. As readable as it is wise."
—*The Junior Bookshelf*

David Lubar

HIDDEN TALENTS

American Library Association
"Best Books for Young Adults"

"Wondrously surprising, playful, and heartwarming." —*VOYA*

"Sure to be popular." —*Kliatt*

Martin Anderson doesn't like being called a loser. But when he ends up at Edgeview Alternative School he has to face the truth: Edgeview is the end of the line. But he discovers something remarkable about himself and his friends: each has a special . . . *hidden* . . . talent.

IN THE LAND OF THE LAWN WEENIES
and other Misadventures

"Four stars!" —*Chicago Tribune*

"Really off the wall stories. They're funny thrillers that scare you out of your seat, but have you laughing all the time."
—Walter The Giant Storyteller

"Clever, creepy, and full of surprises." —James Howe

Kids can be *such* monsters. Literally. From the award-winning author of *Hidden Talents*, two remarkable short story collections— *Kidzilla* and *The Witch's Monkey*—together for the first time. Each hilarious and harrowing.

Roderick MacLeish

PRINCE OMBRA

"Reminiscent of Bradbury's *Something Wicked This Way Comes*."
—*Publishers Weekly*

"Highly recommended."—*Library Journal*

"Whirls the reader along."—*Chicago Sun Times*

Bentley has secret powers. And he's going to need them. Bentley is a hero—the thousand and first to be exact—in a long line of heroes that has stretched all the way back to antiquity. Heroes like Arthur and Hercules. And now: Bentley. One day when Bentley is grown he will be that hero. What Bentley doesn't know is that his "one day" is today.

Caroline Stevermer

A COLLEGE OF MAGICS

"Strikingly set, pleasingly peopled, and cleverly plotted."
—*Kirkus Reviews* (pointer)

"Delightful!"—*The Washington Post*

Teenager Faris Nallaneen—heir to the dukedom of Galazon—is shunted off to Greenlaw College so that her evil uncle can lay claim to her inheritance. But Greenlaw is not just any school as Faris—and her uncle—will soon discover.

Joan Aiken

THE WHISPERING MOUNTAIN

Winner of the Guardian Prize for Fiction

"An enchanting, original story."
—*The Times* of London

In an effort to recover the magical Harp of Teirtu, Owen and his friend Arabis are plunged into a hair-raising adventure of intrigue, kidnapping, exotic underground worlds, savage beasts . . . even murder.

THE SHADOW GUESTS

"Writing seems to be as natural to Joan Aiken as breathing; her imagination is as untrammeled as ever, the precise construction of the astonishing plot lends conviction, and her style is as witty and sparkling with images."
—*The Horn Book*

After the mysterious disappearance of both his mother and older brother, Cosmo is sent away to live with his eccentric mathematician aunt. But things take a weird twist when Cosmo is visited by ghosts from the past. Ghosts who claim to need his help fighting an ancient deadly curse!

THE COCKATRICE BOYS
Illustrated by Gris Grimley

VOYA "Outstanding Science Fiction, Fantasy & Horror Books of the Year"

A plague of monsters has invaded England and Dakin and Sauna come to the rescue! A rollicking comic masterpiece.

Patricia C. Wrede

MAIRELON THE MAGICIAN

"Delightful . . . Wrede's confection will charm readers."
—*Publishers Weekly*

"A wonderful fantasy/mystery. Highly recommended."
—*VOYA*

When street urchin Kim is caught in the act stealing, her accuser surprises her by suggesting she become his apprentice. An apprentice to a magician!

THE MAGICIAN'S WARD

"A sure bet for fans of Philip Pullman's *Ruby in the Smoke* series."
—*VOYA*

Several wizards of Kim's acquaintance have mysteriously disappeared. And it's up to Kim to find out why.